He watched her eyes darken with desire.

Joanna felt so right in his arms....

Suddenly Scott knew that if he wasn't careful, he'd lose control.

Slow, easy, he cautioned himself. He wanted more than a few gentle caresses. He longed to strip her naked and make love to her then and there. But reason told him she wasn't ready for that.

Besides, Tony was sleeping in the next room. What would the boy think if he walked in and found his mother wrapped in the arms of his principal?

Dear Reader,

Welcome to the Silhouette **Special Edition** experience! With your search for consistently satisfying reading in mind, every month the authors and editors of Silhouette **Special Edition** aim to offer you a stimulating blend of deep emotions and high romance.

The name Silhouette **Special Edition** and the distinctive arch on the cover represent a commitment—a commitment to bring you six sensitive, substantial novels each month. In the pages of a Silhouette **Special Edition**, compelling true-to-life characters face riveting emotional issues—and come out winners. All the authors in the series strive for depth, vividness and warmth in writing these stories of living and loving in today's world.

The result, we hope, is romance you can believe in. Deeply emotional, richly romantic, infinitely rewarding—that's the Silhouette **Special Edition** experience. Come share it with us—six times a month!

From all the authors and editors of Silhouette **Special Edition**,

Best wishes,

Leslie Kazanjian,
Senior Editor

MADELYN DOHRN
One for One

Silhouette Special Edition

Published by Silhouette Books New York

America's Publisher of Contemporary Romance

For Anita Diamant—a terrific agent.
Every writer should be so lucky!

SILHOUETTE BOOKS
300 East 42nd St., New York, N.Y. 10017

ISBN: 0-373-09633-X

First Silhouette Books printing November 1990

Printed in the U.S.A.

MADELYN DOHRN

lives in a small Ohio town with her professor husband and family. After years of teaching college English, she decided to try her hand at writing a romance and soon found herself captivated by the task. When she's not in front of her word processor, she likes to travel, read, entertain friends and keep fit with dance-aerobics.

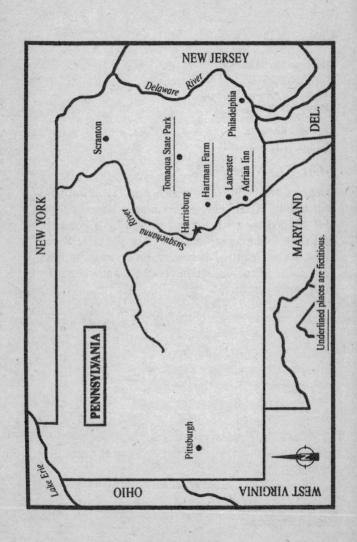

Chapter One

"Mom, I been 'spended!"

Joanna Parker deposited a bag of groceries onto the kitchen counter. Dropping to her knees, she clasped her five-year-old son by his shoulders. She didn't have the foggiest notion what Tony was talking about, but his tone was so grave it sent a ripple of alarm through her. "You've been what?"

"'Spended. Mr. Hartman says so."

"Mr. Hartman? You mean your principal?"

"Yeah. The principal's supposed to be your pal. That's what you said. But he's no pal. He's mean! He 'spended me!"

Joanna's eyes narrowed as it dawned on her what her son was probably talking about. "Do you mean you've been *sus*pended?"

"Yeah. That's it. 'Spended.'" Tony's lower lip drooped in an exaggerated pout.

"But why?"

"He wrote it down." Tony thrust a hand into his pocket and dragged out a tattered piece of paper. "Here."

Rising, Joanna carefully unfolded the note. Words like *misbehaving*, *unruly*, *disobedient* leaped off the page. Within seconds her temper was roiling. "Where's Kathy?" she asked, referring to the fifteen-year-old who sat with Tony until Joanna got home from work.

"In the living room, watching TV. Some mushy thing she taped last night."

For all her anger, Joanna couldn't prevent her lips from tilting upward. Tony's disgruntled tone reflected the typical five-year-old-male attitude toward love and romance. Then her smile wilted as memories swamped her. These past two years she hadn't had much use for Cupid herself.

Spinning on a heel, she marched into the living room where Kathy lay sprawled on her stomach. She was not even blinking—for obvious reasons. The tongue-dueling kiss graphically depicted in twenty-five inches of living color was claiming her undivided attention.

"Kathy, could I talk to you for a minute?"

"Oh, hi, Mrs. Parker." The girl shot Joanna a smile and scrambled to her knees, aiming the remote control at the VCR to switch off the power.

Without preamble, Joanna asked, "What can you tell me about Whittier Elementary's principal?"

"Mr. Hartman? Scott Hartman?"

"That's the one."

"Let me see...." Kathy chewed thoughtfully on her lower lip and rolled her eyes toward the ceiling. "Thick, wavy dark hair. Hazel eyes. Even, white teeth. Gorgeous smile. Sexy walk. A fantastic bod—"

"I wasn't asking for a physical description," Joanna interrupted, unable to disguise her impatience. "What's he like...as a person?"

"Oh." Kathy's gaze remained heavenward, her voice dreamy. "Everybody *loves* Mr. Hartman. I don't know of a girl who went through Whittier who didn't have a crush on him. Me included. One day when I was in fourth grade—" she paused and folded her hands around her arms "—I still get goose bumps when I think about it. Anyway, I was racing for the cafeteria and tripped over my own feet. I'd only twisted my ankle, but I thought it was broken for sure. I was yelling and crying like I was going to die. Mr. Hartman came running out of his office. He looked me over, then picked me up and carried me all the way to the school nurse. He kept smiling at me and telling me I was going to be okay. I can still hear his voice—real deep and gentle."

As Kathy further warmed to her subject, her eyes took on a sparkle. "But the girls weren't his only fans. The guys thought he was great, too. They all wanted to grow up and be like him. I'd say he's at least six-two. And very athletic. I think he was a basketball star in college. Or maybe it was soccer. I don't remember for sure."

Joanna braced her hands on her hips. She'd fully expected Kathy to describe a two-headed, bug-eyed, snaggletoothed monster. In short, an ogre. That the girl had instead sung the man's praises only served to increase Joanna's ire. "Evidently you and I are not on the same wavelength," she said brusquely.

Kathy's mouth dropped open. "Why do you say that?"

"This." Joanna held up the creased letter. "Did Tony say anything to you about Mr. Hartman suspending him?"

The air left Kathy's lungs in a rush. "Not a word."

"Well, he has." Joanna waved the rumpled paper. "If Tony's principal is the Mr. Wonderful you've just painted, then I'd say he suffers from a Jekyll-and-Hyde complex. Otherwise, how could he treat a child like this? And after only four days of classes!"

Kathy gave a helpless shrug. "Maybe there was some mistake. I'm sure Mr. Hartman wouldn't do anything without a good reason."

Though Joanna's opinion differed, she declined to argue the point. No sooner had she sent Kathy on her way than she was reaching for the phone and punching in a number.

"Darlene?" she asked at the "Hello" on the other end of the line. "Joanna Parker here. I'm going to be late getting to the office tomorrow morning. Tony's run into a snag at kindergarten, and I have to stop by the school to straighten it out. It shouldn't take very long. I ought to be at work by ten-thirty."

"Fine," Darlene responded. "Anything I can do to help?"

"No, nothing. But thanks for offering. I'll see you in the morning."

At the dial tone she quickly jabbed out another number. On the fourth ring a voice answered. "Beverly," Joanna said, her nails drumming a nervous tattoo on the slate-topped table, "I've a favor to ask. I was wondering if you could watch Tony all day tomorrow. I'm too upset to talk about why, but Kathy'll explain. Do you think you could manage?" Joanna's sigh of relief was almost audible when her neighbor announced it would be no problem.

Joanna thanked her lucky stars that she had the Jacksons living next door. Three weeks ago she'd been in the middle of unpacking dishes when her buzzer had sounded. She'd found Beverly Jackson standing on her threshold, a homemade pie in one hand, a bouquet of flowers in the other. An hour later, while Beverly helped her arrange pots and pans in the cupboards and chattered on about the different families living in the complex, Joanna knew she'd found a friend for life. And, much to her relief, competent day care for her son. Although Beverly was quite active in the community, she volunteered to watch Tony before school and arranged for her daughter Kathy to keep an eye on him after.

Too bad, Joanna considered as she cradled the phone, her son hadn't had the same luck with his principal! What did they expect of little children these days? Were they to come to school prepared to sit like docile automatons for six hours straight?

Her temper still at a slow boil, she walked to the kitchen where her fingers closed about Hartman's note. Crumpling it into a misshapen ball, she shoved the paper in her pocket.

Joanna spent the night tossing and turning, ransacking her brain for every complaint she intended to level at Scott Hartman. Kathy's praise aside, Joanna had the man pegged. As far as she was concerned, he was a miserable excuse for a principal.

But the following morning, her anger gave way to worry. Over breakfast Tony said very little. The more she prompted, the more he lapsed into silence. Gradually he allowed gestures and facial expressions to supplant words, reminding Joanna of the way he'd reacted to his father's death two years before. So traumatized had Tony been that for nearly twelve months, no sound passed his lips.

Was this disastrous experience with school going to cause him to withdraw again, just when he was gaining some emotional stability? Just when he was beginning to assert himself like any normal, healthy boy?

After gently prodding Tony to finish his cereal and get dressed, Joanna escorted him next door. All the way to Whittier Elementary, she rehearsed how to present her grievance. By the time she was pulling into a visitor's space in front of the building, her temples were pounding.

She threaded her way through the clusters of students milling about in the hall. The shrill childish voices that pierced her ears only exacerbated her headache.

Upon entering the reception area, Joanna found a middle-aged secretary furiously pounding away at a typewriter. When a polite "uh-hmm" didn't catch the woman's attention, Joanna said, "Pardon me."

"Yes?" The secretary, whose nameplate identified her as Mrs. Phyllis Dexter, looked up.

"I'd like to see Mr. Hartman."

"Do you have an appointment?"

"No, but it's urgent."

"Your name?"

"Joanna Parker."

Mrs Dexter eyed her knowingly. "Please have a seat. Mr. Hartman's on the phone, but he should be able to see you in a few minutes."

"Thank you."

Joanna took one of the wooden straight-back chairs and watched the second hand on the clock above the secretary's desk. When it had made five complete sweeps, Joanna started to get antsy. Looking around, she happened to glance at the floor where a shiny new penny lay near the toe of her shoe. In the back of her mind, she could hear her mother's voice: "See a penny, pick it up, all the day, have good luck. See a penny, let it lay, have bad luck all the day."

Joanna didn't like to acknowledge her superstitious streak. Nonetheless, she leaned over and claimed the coin. Just to be on the safe side, she assured herself.

She was surreptitiously slipping the penny into the outside compartment of her purse when Mrs. Dexter announced, "Mr. Hartman's off the phone. You may go in." Striding to the door marked PRINCIPAL, Joanna rapped twice.

"Yes, Phyllis?" As Scott Hartman swiveled around in his big oak chair, his jaw went slack. Instead of his matronly secretary, the most stunning woman he'd ever set eyes on was walking through his doorway. She reminded him of a delicate cameo. Her hair was the color of sun-ripened wheat, her complexion smooth and creamy, her features flawless. What drew him most, though, was her eyes. They were a clear gray and so deep a man could drown in them.

Beautiful eyes, but also troubled.

"What can I do for you?" Scott asked, automatically rising.

"I'm Tony Parker's mother."

"Oh, yes, Mrs. Parker. I'm glad you came in." He forced himself not to stare as he pulled out a chair and motioned her to take it.

Wordlessly, Joanna crossed the room and sat down, then rifled through her purse for the dog-eared note Tony had presented her with the evening before. After unfolding it, she leaned over and laid it before Hartman. "I'm here about this," she said unnecessarily.

"I guessed as much."

"Since my time is valuable, as is yours, I'll get to the point, Mr. Hartman. I'd like a full accounting of the accusations you've made against my son."

Scott tipped his chair back and took a moment to study the woman across from him. Though she was outwardly composed, he sensed an inner turmoil, a turmoil that was reflected not only in her eyes but in the ever-so-slight quaver of her voice. Despite those signs of tension, he decided that she was the type of woman who'd prefer him to be direct.

Straightening, he rested his arms on the desk. "According to his teacher—and my own observations—Tony proved a disruptive element the second he stepped into his kindergarten class."

"That was four days ago. If he was such a problem, why wasn't I contacted earlier?"

"We try to give a child every opportunity to adjust before we take action. Unfortunately, Tony's behavior didn't improve. If anything, it got worse."

Joanna angled her head. "Your letter contained references to his being unruly. Was he deliberately disobedient, or was he simply demonstrating the natural exuberance of a five-year-old?"

"I don't know about you, but I wouldn't define Tony's actions as 'natural exuberance.' He constantly talked—shouted is more accurate—when he was asked to listen, he repeatedly holed up in the boys' lavatory and refused to come out, he threw play dough all around the classroom, he dumped a jar of paint over a classmate's head...." Scott paused. "Shall I go on?"

Joanna's mouth opened and closed, but nothing came out. The child Scott Hartman described was a total stranger, the complete antithesis of the one who'd finally come out of his shell about a year ago. As yet unable to face up to the possibility that her son could be regressing—or worse—she stammered, "A-are you sure we're talking about the same boy?"

"He's the only Tony Parker we have enrolled at Whittier. If he answers to that name, then, yes, I haven't made a mistake."

"But...but why did you send a note home with him? Why didn't you call me if he was giving you so much trouble?"

"We did. First at your home, but there was no answer. And when we tried reaching you at work, all we got was a recorded message that the number we'd dialed wasn't in service."

"How could that be?" Joanna protested.

"Perhaps," he said cautiously, "you made a mistake when you filled out the medical authorization form." At Joanna's skeptical look, Scott stretched out his arm and pressed a button on the intercom. "Phyllis, would you please bring me Tony Parker's file?"

Thirty seconds later the secretary breezed through the door. "Here you are, Mr. Hartman." She spared Joanna a polite smile before leaving.

Scott opened the manila folder and flipped through the pages before plucking out one of several sheets. After scanning it, he said, "According to the information you provided, in case of an emergency we were to notify you at your home phone—555-5901. Or your work number—555-6345."

Joanna closed her eyes and groaned. "You're right. I transposed the last two numbers of the phone where I work. It should be 555-6354." By way of explanation, she added, "I started my new job at Wilkins' Department Store last week, and I guess with the move and all, I got them mixed up." Her gaze dropped to her lap. She'd never felt so foolish in her life.

"That's easy enough to change." Scott wrote in the correction, slipped the form back into the file and tossed it on his desk. "You're new in the community, are you?"

"Yes."

"I couldn't help noticing from the record that you're a single parent."

"Yes," she repeated.

Scott hesitated briefly before delving further. "Does your ex-husband live in the Philadelphia area?" It was his hope that he might be able to enlist the father's help in solving Tony's behavioral problems. From the standpoint of discipline, Scott knew it was essential for parents, even when they were divorced, to present a united front to the child.

"I don't have an ex-husband, Mr. Hartman."

It was Scott's turn to be embarrassed. "I . . . well, I thought you were . . . *Mrs.* Parker."

"I am. But I'm not divorced. I'm a widow." Unbidden, the image of her late husband flashed into Joanna's mind, causing a prickling sensation in her eyes.

"I—I'm sorry," he stammered.

If the man sitting across from her hadn't suspended her son, Joanna would likely have taken pity on him. Scott Hartman was feeling the awkwardness of the moment. Like most people, he hadn't considered the possibility that at her age she could be widowed.

"Thank you," she murmured, "but my marital status isn't the issue here."

"Perhaps it is."

"What do you mean?"

"How long ago did you lose your husband?"

"Two years next month."

Scott rose from his chair, came around to the front of his desk and propped a hip on the corner. "Did he have an accident?"

Joanna directed her gaze to the memo-strewn bulletin board on the wall behind him. "No, he suffered a heart attack."

"I see. Was it unexpected?"

"Totally." As always, whenever Joanna stopped to think about Mike's death, the shock of it still numbed her. She remembered how one second he'd been sitting at the dining room table, slicing into a T-bone steak, and how the next he'd crumpled to the floor.

At first she'd thought some acute pain had seized him, but when her trembling fingers could locate no trace of a pulse, she'd nearly stopped breathing. Only Tony's cries had prevented her from passing out. She'd had to be strong—if not for herself, then for her son.

What followed was a horrid nightmare. Hoping against hope that she was somehow wrong, she'd summoned the rescue squad, who rushed Mike to the hospital, where she paced the emergency-room floor for what seemed hours. Actually, it hadn't taken all that long to have her worst fears confirmed. Her husband was dead. Only later was she told the cause: a massive heart attack.

Rousing herself from the unhappy thoughts, she added, "Mike was so young. We had no inkling he wasn't in perfect health."

Scott reached out to touch her. His fingers closed around her forearm in an expression of sympathy. Though the contact was slight, he was struck by Joanna Parker's fragility. She wasn't a tiny woman, but the delicacy of her bones beneath his fingers surprised him. Their fine structure made her seem all the more vulnerable.

"It must have been very difficult for you," he said, withdrawing his hand. "As well as for Tony. How did he react?"

Joanna blinked back the tears that sprang to her eyes. "In light of how he's behaved at school, you may not believe this, but for a year after Mike's death, he quit talking. He didn't utter a single word."

Scott had to give the woman her due; she'd answered his questions concisely, directly. But the glaze of tears in her eyes gave away stronger, deeper emotions. She said it had been nearly two years, but he suspected that Joanna Parker was still as devastated by her husband's death as her son had been.

Never had Scott been tempted to comfort the mother of one of his students the way he wanted to comfort Joanna. He wanted to do more than give her a consoling pat. He wanted to take her in his arms, stroke a hand up and down her back, whisper that everything was going to be all right. Such actions might be justified as humanitarian, but hardly professional.

Jamming his hands in his pockets, he rounded the desk and again took his seat. "Perhaps Tony's suffered a relapse."

Joanna stretched her palms wide, still not wanting to admit the likelihood to herself. "I don't think so. After all, he's still talking. He clammed up at breakfast, but he did tell me goodbye when I left him with our neighbor."

"When Tony retreated, what brought him out of it?"

"He was seen by a therapist for three months. In layman's terms, Dr. Steiner said that with a lot of love and patience on my part, Tony would adjust. That as soon as he felt secure again, he'd start speaking."

"And he did . . . in about a year, you said."

"That's right."

"During this time, did you go to work?"

"I had no choice." Joanna could have bitten off her tongue at having let slip something so personal. To her, the remark sounded terribly disloyal to Mike. It was as if he hadn't provided for his wife and child in the event of his death. Though Scott sat with his fingers steepled and an expectant look on his face, Joanna's natural reserve prevented her from revealing that the money from Mike's life-insurance policy was safely tucked away in a bank account, earmarked for their son's education.

When she didn't volunteer any further information, Scott cautiously prompted, "Even though you held down a job, you were able to spend time with Tony, weren't you?"

"He was pretty much the center of my life."

Scott arched an eyebrow but said nothing.

Joanna bent forward, her eyes pinning his. "If you're implying that I've been coddling—"

Scott held up his hands. "I didn't mean to sound critical. But think it through, Mrs. Parker. You're advised by a competent therapist to shower your son with love and attention. That this is the one hope of bringing him back to you. And it works." He slid back in his chair. "It seems perfectly logical that Tony had come to expect that when you're home, you devote all your time to him. Would you concede that?"

"I . . . suppose," she said grudgingly, "but—"

Scott didn't allow her to finish. "Have you been able to spend as much time with him these past two weeks as you once did?"

"Three weeks. We moved three weeks ago."

"Three weeks then."

Joanna shrugged. "I suppose not. I had only a week to get our apartment in order. Then because of my promotion, I've had a lot of studying to do—learning new procedures, that sort of thing."

"In other words, Tony's been left to fend for himself."

"I resent that," she said defensively. "I've never gotten home any later than six o'clock since I started this new job. And my son has a sitter both before and after school. He's no latchkey kid. Furthermore, I set up a study at home and do all my extra work there."

"So Tony can entertain himself with you nearby?"

"Yes."

Scott chose his next words carefully. "Doesn't it stand to reason, Mrs. Parker, because you've been distracted by the move and the demands of a new job, Tony would seek to gain your attention by misbehaving?"

"On the contrary, that doesn't make sense. At home he seems perfectly fine. Sometimes a little cranky, but that's it."

"Perhaps Tony's displacing his aggressive behavior."

"That's quite a label for such a little boy. Care to explain?"

"It's my guess Tony's miffed because your job seems to have become more important to you than he is. He'd like to vent his frustration—openly confront you—but he's afraid of displeasing you. Maybe he thinks he'd drive you further away. So what does he do? He substitutes his kindergarten teacher and classmates. It's the classic example of the man wanting to punch out his boss but coming home and kicking the dog instead."

"That's crazy."

"But possible." His eyes were intent upon hers.

Joanna was the first to break contact. She had to admit the man's armchair psychology did make sense. "So what do you suggest?" she asked dismally. "That I put him back in therapy?"

"Not necessarily."

She tilted her head questioningly.

"Tony needs to feel he belongs here. I think he could benefit from becoming involved in one of our community programs. The local Y offers a variety of activities, such as swimming and gymnastics, for kids Tony's age. And the Recreation Department runs a fall sports program. I know for a fact that soccer's quite popular.''

"What makes you think sports would provide the answer?"

"For a five-year-old, Tony's suffered more than his fair share of trauma. First, he loses his father. Then at a particularly critical point in his life—when he starts school—he's uprooted and thrust into a new environment where he doesn't know anyone. Worse yet, his mother isn't able to spend as much time with him as she once was." When Joanna would have spoken, Scott held up a staying hand. "Hold on, now. I'm not finding fault, just stating a fact. Everybody assumes children are so resilient, yet change can produce as much anxiety in them as it does in adults. Exercise is a terrific antidote to stress. Not only that, but if Tony went out for some team sport like soccer, he'd be able to learn to work with a group. If he can do that on a playing field, he'll have better luck relating to his peers in the classroom."

Joanna bit her inner lip. It had crossed her mind that the timing for this move had been wrong. But the step up to administrative assistant had seemed an answer to her prayers. She'd dropped out of college after her freshman year to marry Mike, and as a secretary she'd had trouble making ends meet for her and Tony. With the new position came a hefty raise, one she couldn't afford to turn down. Plus, she'd be getting away from her former boss, Dwayne Simmons, whose persistent attempts to win her affection had become more and more offensive.

Though Joanna had worried that relocating to Philadelphia might unsettle her son, she'd told herself that after recovering from his father's death, he was strong enough to take the move in stride. Obviously she'd been wrong.

Now, sitting in the principal's office, Joanna felt a stab of guilt. If she'd focused more on Tony and less on herself, he wouldn't be having such a time of it.

But she'd cast her lot and there was no turning back.

"I'll talk to Tony and see what he thinks about your suggestions. I wouldn't want to force him into something he wasn't interested in doing."

"Of course not. But if I were you, I'd strongly urge him to participate." Scott reached for a pad and pencil. "Here's the Recreation Department's number. Ask for Phil Matthews. He's in charge of the program and will tell you how to sign Tony up." He snapped his fingers as if another thought had just occurred to him. "Something else I should mention while you're here— the school's One-for-One Club."

"Oh?"

"I think this is something else Tony could profit from. The faculty members at Whittier help out new students on an individual basis. They introduce them to the other kids, sometimes eat with them in the cafeteria—that sort of thing. The teachers even take the children on special outings, so they learn about the community and don't feel like the new kids on the block for long."

"Why haven't I heard about this club before?"

"You will. Tomorrow. We wait a week to make sure enrollment has stabilized, then we send out letters to the parents, giving them information and inviting them to an organizational meeting. Notices went out today. The meeting will be Monday night."

"I see."

"In the meantime, I'll arrange to have Tony placed in one of our special classes where he'll get lots of individual attention. I don't think it'll be too long before he's ready to return to Mrs. Drummond's room."

"Mr. Hartman—" Joanna got to her feet, offering him her hand and a faint smile "—I want to thank you for seeing me on such short notice."

Scott's large hand nearly swallowed up Joanna's much smaller one. "That's my job. If all parents were as concerned about their offspring as you are, we wouldn't have any discipline problems."

Joanna lowered her gaze, suddenly aware of his touch. When at last he released her hand, she brought her eyes to his. For the first time she noticed what an intriguing shade they were—not brown and not green, but a curious combination. What captivated her most, though, was the kindness that emanated from their depths.

"Don't worry, Mrs. Parker. Tony's going to be fine. You'll see." When she failed to respond, he continued, "Last year a mother came in a few days before school, all upset because her daughter seemed to have regressed to the terrible twos—constantly crying, throwing temper tantrums. She'd even reverted to baby talk and sucking her thumb." Scott's smile was aimed to reassure. "Not many days after school began, that same mother stopped by to tell me her little girl was back to normal. So you see, Mrs. Parker, Tony's problems aren't unusual."

Joanna cleared her throat. "Thank you again, Mr. Hartman. For everything. I suppose I'll see you at the One-for-One meeting."

"If not before," he responded cryptically.

Chapter Two

That evening Joanna ordered in Tony's favorite meal—pizza with extra cheese and mounds of pepperoni. She was somewhat cheered that he was once again talking instead of answering her questions with signals and monosyllables. Evidently his day with Beverly had done him a world of good. But then her neighbor was the sort who could coax conversation from a cigar-store Indian.

While battling the stringy mozzarella, Joanna broached the subject of her conference with his principal. "Tony, why didn't you tell me what you were doing in school?"

"Whatcha mean, Mom?"

"I'm talking about your conduct." In a voice that was both firm and gentle, she said, "You were giving your teacher and some of your classmates fits, weren't you? Doing things that were naughty. Even unkind and downright mean.'' Joanna made a distinction—as she always did—between the act and the child. She never disapproved of Tony, only of his behavior.

''I guess,'' he admitted sheepishly.

''Why do you suppose you were misbehaving?''

He avoided her eyes and hunched his small shoulders. ''Don't know.''

Joanna refused to let him off the hook but went directly to the heart of the matter. ''Are you mad at me, Tony?''

He bit off a mouthful of pizza, taking his time chewing and swallowing before he answered. ''Maybe I am. A little.''

''Do you think I'm neglecting you because of my new job?''

Tony took a long pull on his root beer. Reaching for another slice of pizza, he evaded his mother's steady gaze. ''You're always studying your books.''

''Does that make you think I'd rather spend time reading my training manuals than with you?'' When Tony didn't reply, Joanna knew Scott Hartman had been right. The child was feeling rejected.

She cupped his chin with her hands and tenderly tipped his face toward hers. ''Don't you know you're the most important thing in the world to me? Don't you know how much I love you?''

''I s'pose.''

''No supposing about it. Nothing or no one could mean more to me than you do.'' She watched his face brighten and was filled with a sense of relief. "Let's make a deal, okay?"

"Okay."

"When I get home from work, I won't head for my study until after you're in bed. Would you like that?"

His mouth curved from ear to ear, and his head bobbed vigorously.

"In return, I want you to agree to something. When I was talking to Mr. Hartman—"

"Mr. Hartman," Tony grumbled. "Yuck!"

"Tony, I'll not have you showing lack of respect for your principal."

"But he's mean. He 'spended me."

"*Sus*pended," Joanna corrected automatically. "That doesn't make him mean. He did what he thought was best for the other children. And, I might add, for you."

Tony wrinkled his nose and emitted a childish grunt. He looked so endearingly skeptical that Joanna had to stifle a laugh.

"Yes, you." She poured dressing on her salad. "He said you might enjoy taking part in the local sports program."

"Do they have football?"

His easy capitulation surprised Joanna. "I don't know. Mr. Hartman didn't mention it specifically, though he did talk about soccer."

"Soccer," Tony pronounced with disdain. "If I play anything, I wanna play football. Dad was a great football player."

Joanna reached over and brushed a shock of sandy hair off his forehead. "I know." The yearbooks that Tony frequently leafed through pictured Mike in all his glory—jumping into the air to snag passes with the tips of his fingers, dodging through burly linemen to gain yardage, leaping over a pileup of players to score touchdowns. When it came to football, Mike had done it all. She'd always considered it odd that a man who was such a perfect physical specimen could die of a heart attack.

Joanna thrust aside the memories of Mike and placed a hand over her son's. "I wouldn't hurt your feelings for the world, Tony, but you take more after my family, and we're not exactly built for football."

"I don't care."

"In that case, I promise to look into it for you," she hedged.

Fortunately, Joanna didn't have to do battle with her son. The following morning when she spoke with Phil Matthews, she learned that boys had to be at least nine before they could participate in midget football. But, the director was quick to note, the department did sponsor the Tornadoes, a soccer team for children ages five to seven. The first practice was being held that very afternoon, and he assured her Tony could take part, even though he wasn't officially registered.

While Tony wasn't as elated as he might have been if he were going out for football, he was, nevertheless, excited. Normally the Saturday cartoons kept him fairly well entertained, but not that morning.

Joanna was in the middle of whipping up a cake when Tony dashed into the kitchen. "This okay, Mom?" he asked, turning around as if he were modeling the latest in soccer fashion.

"Fine, except for the foot gear." She nodded toward the new tennis shoes they'd just purchased for school. "Why don't you wear your old pair? That way you won't risk messing up the new ones."

"They're full of holes," Tony complained.

"One," Joanna corrected.

"But it's a big hole."

"Oh, yes. About the size of your thumbnail."

Realizing his mother wasn't about to budge, Tony at last surrendered. "Okay," he said, his chin touching his chest.

Joanna smiled indulgently, though she couldn't hear what he mumbled under his breath as he trudged out of the kitchen.

Joanna's upside-down cake took longer to bake than she had anticipated, but by driving a shade faster than the speed limit and catching the tail end of several green lights, she got Tony to the field with two minutes to spare.

Together they sprinted across the parking lot. Since the warm days of August had extended into September, Joanna's brow was filmed with perspiration by the time they reached the practice area. They slowed to a walk while she struggled to catch her breath.

One look told her that about twenty boys and girls—of assorted sizes and shapes—comprised the Tornadoes. With the exception of the youngest, the obvious rookies, they were running around shouting and carrying on, each trying to outdo the other.

The team was appropriately tagged, Joanna concluded. They were tornadoes, all right! Volatile, tempestuous, boisterous. She pitied their coach. Anyone who'd take on a bunch this wild had to be a saint.

By some miracle, an adult voice managed to boom out over the on-field racket. It belonged to a tall, rangy man standing in the middle of the unruly pack. His back was to Joanna, and he was calling out names from the list attached to his clipboard.

Joanna rested her hand at the base of Tony's neck and steered him in the direction of the coach. She wanted to explain that he wouldn't find her son on his roster but that she planned to stop in at the Recreation Department's office on Monday and get him officially registered.

"Excuse me, sir," Joanna spoke up, at the same time tapping the coach's shoulder to gain his attention. When he wheeled about, she gasped in surprise.

Scott Hartman turned his warm hazel eyes on her. For a few seconds their gazes held. Then he angled his head to greet her son. "Tony, I'm glad you could make it."

Despite the friendliness in his principal's voice, Tony's face crumpled and his gaze fell to his feet. "Why're you here?"

Scott hunkered down so the boy had no choice but to look directly at him. He held out a stopwatch in one hand and a shiny whistle in the other. "I'm the coach."

Tony glared at his mother accusingly. With a pang Joanna tried to ignore his unspoken message.

"Mr. Hartman," she said, projecting her voice as much as she could without actually screaming. "I had no idea you were in charge."

"Hey, guys," Scott bellowed, though not unkindly, at the group. "Try to get it down to a dull roar, will you? I can't hear myself think." He took Joanna by the elbow and led her a short distance away. "For the last three years the Tornadoes have been my team."

"Why didn't you say so yesterday afternoon?"

"Because I figured you'd tell Tony. I was afraid he might not want to join if he knew I'd be his coach." Scott looked over his shoulder, where the boy's hands were shoved in his pockets, his head still bowed. He was digging an imaginary hole in the ground with the toe of his tennis shoe. "He doesn't look too happy, does he?"

"No," Joanna admitted worriedly, then stiffened her spine. "But I think you're right. He needs to learn to get along with children his age, to feel he belongs. And, like all of us, he could use a healthy outlet for his frustrations." She bit worriedly on her lower lip. "This is all my fault. I shouldn't have moved just before he started school. One or the other would have been enough for him to cope with. But both!"

"Don't heap too much blame on your shoulders." Scott's gaze traveled briefly over the knit fabric of her green tank top. He wanted to add that they were much too slim to bear such burdens. And much too pretty. Instead, he assured her, "And try not to worry. It may take a while, but Tony and I are going to get along fine."

Before she could utter a single word, he patted her arm and jogged back toward the group, giving three sharp blasts on his whistle. At the signal to settle down to business, the Tornadoes clustered around him.

All, that is, except Tony, who stood looking daggers at his mother. She could almost read his mind. He thought she'd sold out to the enemy. Though her son's obvious distress hurt, she couldn't allow herself to soften and relent.

She pivoted and headed toward the bleachers, where several other parents were seated.

" . . . Free at last," she overheard a sultry feminine voice about three rows behind her announce.

Joanna turned her head just enough to catch the attractive brunette's broad smile as she wiggled the unadorned ring finger of her left hand.

"When was your divorce final, Abby?" asked the woman beside her.

"Ten o'clock this morning."

"Hmm. Right in time for soccer season. Lucky you. Especially since Scott Hartman's still unattached."

"I couldn't have put it better myself," Abby purred. "He's one gorgeous hunk of a man, isn't he?"

"You can say that again," her companion agreed. "Why'd you wait this long to make your move? You and Stan separated last spring."

"Because Hartman's much too straight. I kept my fingers crossed that he wouldn't find someone until I was available." Abby giggled. "I got my wish and now..." Her voice lowered to a conspiratorial whisper as she shared her scheme with the other woman.

Sitting on the bottom row, Joanna could barely restrain herself from twisting around to get a better look at this Abby creature who planned to sink her long red nails into Scott Hartman. She wondered how he'd feel if he knew about the woman's intentions. Angry? Amused? Flattered? For a brief instant, she flirted with the idea of warning him, but immediately rejected the notion. She wouldn't dare intrude on his personal life. At best, he was an acquaintance, not a friend.

Anyway, Joanna sniffed, if Principal Hartman wanted to become involved with someone as openly brazen as Abby, that was his business. She had quite enough to do to mind her own.

Joanna had no trouble putting aside the temptation to play busybody. But she didn't have such an easy time dismissing the woman's assessment of Scott as a "gorgeous hunk." Yesterday she'd been too shaken, today too stunned to take full measure of the man. Now she did. Slowly. Thoroughly. She had to agree with Abby. Even in a T-shirt and baggy sweat pants, he was nice to look at. He had a long, lean, broad-shouldered build she found attractive, and a loose-hipped way of moving that was sexy enough to make a woman's mouth water.

As she watched Scott separate the youngsters into groups, a faint quiver stirred within her.

Joanna's gasp was nearly audible. Not since Mike's death had she experienced anything remotely resembling desire, but the signs were unmistakable. Determinedly, she beat back the response. She wasn't emotionally prepared for another relationship. After what she had shared with Mike, then lost, she doubted she ever would be.

Instead of ogling Scott's wonderful physique, for the next hour she concentrated on the way he handled his small charges. How he could bring order to all that chaos, she'd never know, but somehow he was managing—like a gifted sculptor giving form to a shapeless lump of clay. Her opinion of his character went up at least three notches.

First off, he ran the kids around the perimeter of the field several times. To loosen them up, Joanna supposed. Next, he stood them in line, then rolled the ball toward each child, who was instructed to charge and kick it back to him. Following that little exercise, he had them try dribbling the ball with their feet. As uncoordinated as most were, the workout resembled a scene from a Keystone Cops movie more than soccer practice. It was all Joanna could do to maintain a straight face. Yet Scott, she noticed, never laughed, but encouraged the children with constant words of praise.

"Mr. Hartman's good with them, isn't he?" Joanna found herself remarking to the couple seated not far from her.

"He sure is," the woman responded. "This is our daughter's third year to play under him." She squinted thoughtfully. "I haven't seen you around before. Your child just starting?"

"Yes. My son. We recently moved to the area from New York."

"City or state?"

"City."

"Welcome to Philadelphia. By the way, I'm Claire Richards, and this—" she placed a hand on the arm of the man sitting next to her "—is my husband, Gary."

After Joanna had introduced herself, Claire asked, "Which one's your boy?"

Joanna pointed toward the field. "Tony's in the tan top and navy shorts."

"He around five?"

"Yes. He'll be six next month."

Claire smiled. "They're so cute at that age. And so funny. They take everything quite seriously... and literally. I remember the first game our Shelly played. Mr. Hartman planted her on a spot and told her that she was to guard her particular territory, emphasizing she wasn't to stray out of it. Well, we weren't two minutes into the game when the ball came within a foot of her, but Shelly didn't budge an inch. Just let it roll right on by. Seems she thought she should move only if it landed right on top of her feet!"

"If I'd been Hartman," Gary put in, "I'd've chewed her out but good."

"Oh, sure. You talk big. If he'd said one word to ruffle your little girl, you'd have been ready to deck him. But you are right about one thing, dear," Claire tacked on. "You'd make a lousy coach. You don't have the patience."

This time Gary must have agreed with his wife because he offered no further comment. Joanna's eyes strayed back to the playing field. She imagined Mike out there trying to corral twenty kids. By now he'd have been tearing his hair out and barking orders at the top of his lungs. Her husband had had his share of virtues, but patience wasn't one of them. He was much too aggressive to keep his cool.

By contrast, Scott Hartman seemed to be in complete control. If he had a temper, he never let it surface. He worked with the children in a way Joanna could only admire. He was firm, but scrupulously fair.

At the end of sixty minutes, he blew his whistle to signal the end of practice. The Tornadoes came whirling off the field, happy and excited. All but Tony. He slogged toward Joanna as though he were wading knee deep in mud. An icy fear gripped her middle. She'd counted on his lightening up a bit and having a good time.

Fashioning a smile, she ran her fingers through Tony's light brown hair. She was about to suggest they stop somewhere for a root beer when Gary Richards offered to treat the whole gang to ice-cream cones at the neighborhood dairy twist.

"Would you like that, Tony?"

Before he could reply, a deep voice asked, "You know how to get to the Double Dipper?"

Joanna hadn't noticed Scott come up behind her. She swung her head to the side. "No," she answered, a bit unnerved by his nearness.

"It's tricky to find, so why don't you and Tony ride with me? I can drop you back here to pick up your car when we're finished."

Once again Joanna felt trapped. She couldn't insult Scott by refusing his offer; at the same time she didn't relish disturbing Tony any further by accepting. In the end, she left the choice in her son's hands. "What do you say, Tony? Shall we hitch a ride with Mr. Hartman?"

The boy's dilemma was written all over his face. He didn't want to chance losing out on an ice-cream cone in case his mother got lost. But he wasn't any too happy about keeping company with his principal. For a time he seemed to weigh the decision, but at last he nodded. "Okay."

As it turned out, Scott's recreational van was parked right next to Joanna's compact. Tony's eyes sparkled as he climbed into the back, his anger with his principal momentarily forgotten. "Do you go camping in this?"

"Sometimes. Tomaqua State Park isn't far from here. It's probably my favorite spot." He took Joanna by the arm and helped her in on the passenger side.

Tony scooted across the seat. "What're these?" He lifted several strands of long, dark hair.

"They must have come from Miss Kitty."

Joanna sucked in her breath. Before she could tell her son to mind his business, he blurted, "Who's she?"

Scott tossed the boy a lopsided grin and helped him fasten his seat belt. "A very special lady—my cat."

Joanna coughed to hide her sigh of relief.

"You have a cat?" Tony went on.

"Sure do."

"I want a dog, but Mom won't let me have one."

"Now, Tony," Joanna admonished gently, trying to get her wayward imagination under control. "You know very well we can't have a dog when we live in an apartment. It wouldn't be fair. Dogs need space to run and play."

Scott rounded the front of the van and settled himself behind the wheel. "Your mom's right, Tony. Dogs require a lot of room—and attention. That's why I have a cat."

"I wouldn't want a cat."

"Don't be too quick to judge. Miss Kitty just might win you over. She's nosy—like most members of her species. Ever hear the saying, 'Curiosity killed the cat'? On the other hand, I could swear she's half dog." Scott caught the boy's doubtful scowl in the rearview mirror and added, "She likes to retrieve."

Tony's eyes widened. "Fetch a ball? No fooling?"

"No fooling." Twisting the key in the ignition, Scott glimpsed over his shoulder. "When I toss her a rubber ball, she'll chase after it. She likes to bat it around awhile, but eventually she brings it back to me. If I put my hand down, she'll drop it right in my palm, then sit back and wait until I throw it again."

"I never saw a cat do that."

"Neither did I. Until I found Miss Kitty."

"You found her?"

"About five years ago," Scott said as he put the van in gear and eased out of the parking space. "She'd been wandering around the neighborhood for a couple of days. I finally realized she was a stray and took her in. Originally I planned to feed her and drop her off at the animal shelter. But when I discovered what a character she is, I decided to keep her.''

"I suppose she's a lot of company for you," Joanna inserted.

"Yes, it's nice to have someone waiting at home."

Joanna thought she caught a touch of wistfulness in the admission but immediately decided she'd been mistaken.

"Does she sleep with you?" Tony piped up.

"No, she has her own bed. But I wouldn't mind if she did. Particularly on a cold night."

"Fuzzy sleeps with me."

"Fuzzy?"

"My bear. Grandma and Grandpa Mansfield gave him to me."

"It's nice having something soft and warm to curl up with, isn't it?"

Out of the corner of her eye, Joanna glanced at Scott and once more wondered if he was talking exclusively about teddies and cats. She couldn't tell. His eyes were on the road, his expression utterly guileless. Perhaps she was reading too much into his words. No doubt Abby's fault. Even so, she couldn't prevent her pulse from quickening.

Tony kicked his legs back and forth in a heedless rhythm. "I wish I could play with Miss Kitty sometime."

"I think that could be arranged." Scott's gaze flickered toward Joanna. "If it's okay with your mother."

"We'll see," she said, not at all certain why she was feeling so put out.

Chapter Three

Joanna's heart leaped to her throat at the loud sizzle coming from the engine of her car. It sounded as if someone were frying eggs on the manifold. Carefully, she pulled alongside the curb. After popping the release lever, she got out and raised the hood. What she knew about cars would fit on a computer chip. But she didn't have to be a mechanical wizard to discover her problem. A hose had split and spewed liquid—water? antifreeze?—all over the engine.

"Damn," she swore uncharacteristically. She'd been running behind as it was. Now she was going to be walking into the One-for-One meeting after it had already started. If she didn't miss it completely.

Exasperated, Joanna looked around. Fortunately the hose had blown in a residential area rather than on the freeway, so she'd be able to call a garage. But which house should she approach?

The cozy two-story frame in front of her was inviting. With a gabled roof, decorative cornices, shuttered bay windows and shell-pink trim, it resembled, to Joanna's way of thinking, something straight out of "Hansel and Gretel."

She moved her feet in the direction of the gingerbread house, trusting that the lady in residence bore no resemblance to the wicked witch of German folklore.

"The purpose of the One-for-One Club," Scott informed the parents seated around tables in Whittier's cafeteria, "is to serve as a bridge between school and community, particularly for newcomers. So please let your children know which staff member they've been paired with." His eyes briefly skimmed the adult leaders present. "Tell them they'll eat lunch with that teacher or administrator tomorrow and together they'll be planning some outings. Also encourage them to look upon their advocate as a friend, someone they can go to with any problems they may encounter at school. The quicker they feel a part of the system, the better off they're going to be."

Scott's eyes took a final tour of the pleasant faces surrounding him. When he didn't locate the one he'd been looking for all evening, he remarked, "If there are no further questions, we'll adjourn. I want to thank all of you for coming and for taking such an active interest in your children."

Though Scott meant what he said, his voice struck him as hollow. He couldn't begin to measure his disappointment that Joanna Parker had not attended this initial session. Last Friday—and again on Saturday—he'd have staked his life on the belief she was the kind of mother who would be committed to helping her son over the rough spots. That he'd been wrong about her came as a surprise.

It also caused him a sharp pang of regret.

Glumly, Scott watched the meeting break up. He wasn't sure whether he felt let down because he'd badly misjudged Joanna or because all day he'd keenly anticipated seeing her again. After everyone had left, he walked over to the refreshment table and filled a cup with tepid coffee.

Buck up, Hartman, he lectured himself. *This isn't the first time you've been wrong about a parent . . . or, for that matter, a woman.*

He made a face when he took a sip of the bitter dregs. Tossing the cup into the trash, he gathered up the sheaf of papers he'd used during the organizational meeting and was thrusting the hodgepodge into his briefcase when Joanna burst through the door.

"Good, you're still here," she said, panting. When she'd recovered enough to glance around, she suddenly became aware that the two of them were alone. "Oh, no! The meeting's over, isn't it?"

"Umm," Scott grunted noncommittally, his expression blank.

"Well," Joanna ventured when he failed to elaborate, "what happened?"

"If you wanted to know, you should have been here—" he glanced at his watch "—about an hour ago."

At the icy tone in Scott's voice, Joanna's temper flared. He had no idea what she'd gone through simply to try to make the tail end of this meeting! Without giving her a chance to explain, he'd jumped to the conclusion that she'd been purposely late!

Incensed at the injustice of it all, she shot him a murderous look. "I don't need this!"

"No, I don't suppose you do," he countered mildly. "How kind of you to understand."

The sparks in Joanna's eyes were wicked enough to touch off a four-alarm fire, but Scott refused to be her timber. As far as he was concerned, heated words never accomplished much, particularly with an irate parent. Right now, Joanna Parker would profit more from sound advice then angry reproach.

"Your son," he patiently recounted, "has problems. You led me to believe that helping him overcome them was your top priority...." His voice trailed off.

She glared at him. "Exactly why do you think I was late, Mr. Hartman? Because I was trying to earn Brownie points by working overtime? Or easing the tensions of a hard day at the office with a few drinks at some singles bar?"

Scott shut the clasps on his briefcase. Forcefully. "You don't owe me any explanations."

"That's right. I don't. You're Tony's principal. Not my—" The words tumbled to a halt.

Her near slip had an instant sobering effect. Pulling in a deep breath, Joanna slumped onto a chair. "Look, Mr. Hartman, I've had a rough day and I'm taking my frustration out on you. I apologize. I'm usually not this short with people, but after a rather weird—" She broke off again and rubbed her temples. "Forgive me. I'm not quite myself."

"Don't you feel well?" Scott asked, suddenly concerned.

She smiled wanly, touched by the warmth in his voice. "I'm fine—just tired. I only wish I *were* coming down with something. It would be a convenient excuse for flying off the handle the way I did."

Scott studied her more carefully. She did look beat. And terribly vulnerable. He resisted an urge to put his arm around her shoulders and comfort her, throwing her a cocky grin instead. "Could be hoof-in-mouth disease."

"What?"

His hazel eyes twinkled with mischief. "I believe you're suffering from hoof-in-mouth disease. A classic case if ever I've seen one."

Joanna frowned. "I beg your pardon?"

"On the farm where I grew up, we inoculated animals against hoof-and-mouth disease. Hoof *and* mouth—hoof *in* mouth. You follow?" At her puzzled expression, Scott swiped the air with a palm. "I guess it loses something in translation."

Feeling foolish when at last she did catch on to the joke, Joanna gave a dry chuckle. "I'm a little slow on the uptake tonight, but I think I get your point. In the future I'll try to keep my foot away from my mouth."

His smile was forgiving. "Nobody's perfect."

"In case you're interested, I do have a good reason for missing the meeting. I had car trouble."

He raised an eyebrow.

"I know that's one of those tired old clichés—like the check's in the mail—but honest—" she put a hand to her heart "—my car did break down. And that's only the half of it."

Curious, Scott straddled a chair and rested his arms across the back. "I'm listening."

"I met the most bizarre person."

"How bizarre? Enough to frighten you?"

"No. I'm sure the woman's harmless. With her curly blue hair and rouged cheeks she looks like a cherubic grandmother. Plus she's so frail a puff of wind could blow her away." Joanna's eyes rounded. "It wasn't so much her appearance as her behavior—you wouldn't believe this woman!"

"Try me," Scott urged, further intrigued by Joanna's expressive face. Now that he had her here, he wasn't eager to let her go.

"She calls herself Hecate."

"Like the witch in *Macbeth*?"

Joanna nodded. "That's what she fancies herself."

"A witch? Come on!"

"Scout's honor."

Scott eyed her dubiously. "I hear all kinds of excuses for tardiness. But this! You're making it up."

"I most certainly am not!"

He lifted his shoulders as if he were humoring a child. "I'm all ears."

"My car broke down on Decatur Street. You remember 'Hansel and Gretel'?"

"Yes," he said, uncertain that he'd ever be able to make sense out of Joanna's rambling tale, but at this point he didn't care. Joanna Parker was enchanting to watch with her wide-set silver eyes and pale gold hair and long stockinged legs so primly crossed beneath the table. He could hardly believe she was the same serious, no-nonsense woman he'd met a few days ago. Tonight she seemed almost whimsical. He hadn't figured her for the mischievous sort, but whatever she was up to, he was willing to play along. For the time being. Folding his arms across his chest, Scott remarked blandly, "I was once a child."

Joanna disregarded the good-natured jibe and went on with her story. "Well, this house looks exactly like the wicked witch's—it's so snug and cute and inviting."

"So you thought it was safe to ring the bell and ask to use the phone," he concluded.

"Right. Hecate invited me in, and I called a garage."

"That's it? Shoot!" He appeared woefully disappointed. "I expected you to say she jumped on her broomstick and offered to fly you to the nearest repair shop."

"That came later."

"Now you *are* putting me on."

"Not at all. After I'd waited thirty minutes without the tow truck showing up, she did hint her broomstick was much faster."

Scott laughed, holding up a hand. "Enough! I surrender."

She rewarded him with a bright smile. "Then you believe me?"

"Let's say I've been sufficiently sidetracked."

"But I haven't come to the best part yet."

He groaned. "There's more?"

Joanna nodded and hooked a strand of hair behind her ear. "Hecate insisted upon telling my fortune. I didn't want her to. You see—" she gestured with up-turned palms "—how should I say this? I'm a bit . . . suggestible."

Scott threw her a crooked grin. "How suggestible?"

"Let me put it this way. I make it a point never to read my horoscope until the day after."

"A wise habit, I'm sure, but probably scant defense against a woman like Hecate. Don't tell me she pulled the old crystal-ball shtick on you."

"No crystal ball, no tarot cards, no tea leaves. Those are gypsy props. Hecate's a witch. There's a distinction. She mixed up a brew from some bottles she keeps in an old wooden medicine chest." At the skeptical slant of his mouth, Joanna protested, "Well, she did! Eye of newt, toe of frog, wool of bat, tongue of dog. Sound familiar?"

"I hate to admit this, but those ingredients do ring a bell."

"*Macbeth.*"

"Of course!" Dramatically, Scott smacked a fist against his forehead. "How could I have forgotten the obvious? You're lucky she didn't suggest you swallow that concoction. The woman sounds decidedly bonkers."

"Eccentric's more accurate. At any rate, she stirred the conglomeration up, studied it a while, then told me what the future held in store."

"Let me guess. A tall, dark, handsome stranger's going to come into your life and sweep you off your feet."

Joanna couldn't suppress a laugh. "How did you know?"

"Doesn't the standard fortune always include a tall, dark, handsome stranger?" Scott hiked a shoulder. "I suppose he represents every woman's dream."

"You can say that again." Joanna colored at the full import of her words. To cover her embarrassment, she plunged on. "Actually, my handsome stranger's supposed to be blond and blue-eyed."

Scott's voice was low. "I prefer my description."

Looking at the rugged man before her, Joanna suddenly found oxygen in the room scarce. She licked her lips and rapidly changed the subject. "Anyhow, the tow truck finally showed up and hauled my car to the garage, where I left it. It won't get fixed until tomorrow. And by the time I called a cab and got over here, I missed the meeting." She gave Scott a small smile. "That, Mr. Principal, is my excuse. Will you let me off the hook? Or do I get detention?"

Rubbing his beard-shadowed jaw, Scott rose, hitched a hip on the corner of the table and looked down at Joanna. "I'll let you off. This time. But only because I'm convinced you couldn't have invented anything as flaky as that tale."

Joanna smiled. "Thanks for the vote of confidence. I really do operate on all four cylinders. Which is more than I can say for my car. So tell me, what did I miss at the meeting?"

"Nothing much you don't already know. Except for the name of the person who'll be helping Tony out for the next six or eight weeks."

"And I did so want to meet his advocate. Who is it?"

Scott jiggled the change in his pants pocket. "Three guesses."

"Since I hardly know any of the faculty members, I'll have to pass."

Summoning up his best professional tone, Scott stated, "I don't see any point in keeping you in the dark. I'm the one who'll be working with Tony."

"You? But . . . but I thought only teachers were involved in One-for-One."

"Normally that's the case. But this year's a little different. With the big East-Tech Electronics plant opening up this summer, enrollment in the district has soared. Until the situation eases, Mr. Stone, our new superintendent, asked that administrators also participate."

"I see." Joanna looked directly at Scott. How was she going to worm her way out of this tight spot? She could well imagine Tony's reaction when he learned that his principal would be his One-for-One partner.

To be honest, she herself found Scott Hartman enormously appealing. Like last Saturday at the Double Dipper when Abby What's-her-name had thrown herself at him. The woman had come on so strong that no one would have blamed him had he bluntly rebuffed her advances. Instead, he'd let her down easy. While he'd made certain Abby knew he wasn't interested, he'd done it in so teasing a manner that he hadn't wounded her ego.

Joanna had been enormously impressed. And, though she was reluctant to admit it, pleased.

But Tony didn't share his mother's esteem. The burst of animation he'd displayed over Scott's van and pet cat had soon evaporated. By the time they'd finished their ice-cream cones, Tony had again shrunk back into his shell. Despite Scott's efforts to draw him out, he hadn't had much to say, giving only a "yes" or "no" when he was spoken to.

Joanna felt as if she were between a rock and a hard place. At the same time that she wanted to help Tony, she also wanted to spare Scott's feelings. Popular as he was, it must be an ego-deflating experience to find himself in the position of trying to win someone over— above all a student.

"I know what you're wondering," Scott said.

"You do?"

"Yeah. How I ended up being paired with Tony."

Actually, Joanna hadn't given a thought to that, but now that Scott mentioned it, she was curious. "How did you?"

His mouth turned up in a half smile. "The luck of the draw, though I don't suppose your Miss Hecate would buy that. Anyhow, Mr. Stone randomly matched up each student with a staff member, so it was strictly coincidence Tony was assigned to me. If I thought it would do any good, I'd go to Stone and ask that he make a switch. But—and I hope you agree with me—that would only be putting the problem on a back burner, and I think it needs to be addressed now. Even if Tony doesn't come to like me, he can at least learn to tolerate me. To trust me."

"I—I'm not . . ." She shrugged helplessly.

"You don't have to spare my feelings. Since I was the one to bar Tony from his kindergarten class, he considers me bad news. I can understand that. For a time there on Saturday, I thought I was making some headway. But no sooner had he thawed out a little than he froze up again."

"I noticed," Joanna allowed, following Scott's lead to be candid.

He raked a hand through his dark hair. "Did Tony happen to let on why? Or did you ask?"

"I tried to feel him out, but he didn't offer much. He spent a good bit of time in his room, fighting one of his medieval battles."

"Medieval battles?"

Joanna gave a little laugh. "It's not as violent as it sounds. You see, Mike—my husband—played a lot of chess. He had several sets with intricately carved pieces. After he died, Tony would take them out and play with them by the hour. They seemed to serve as a link to his father. I think he subconsciously believed that as long as he could touch something tangible of Mike's..." She shook her head. "It's just my own crazy theory."

"It has merit."

"After a while, Tony got out the chess pieces less and less frequently. Until this past weekend he hadn't played with them for months. I don't need a psychologist to tell me our move has set Tony off. If there were some way I could turn back the clock—"

"But you can't." Vaguely Scott wondered, would she if she really could? Had Joanna and Tony not come to Philadelphia, he'd never have met her. But perhaps she wouldn't see that as any great loss. Maybe he was the only one feeling this indefinable pull between them.

Scott braced an arm on his leg. "I've said this before, but it bears repeating. Don't waste time worrying. Tony and I will eventually make our peace. Tomorrow I'll have lunch with him and we'll decide on an outing for the weekend. He seems to like animals. You think he might enjoy a trip to the zoo Sunday afternoon?"

"A few weeks ago I'd have said yes without the slightest hesitation. But now I can't vouch for Tony's reaction. He might take to the suggestion, but then again, he might not."

"Are you trying to tell me he'd be more likely to enjoy himself if I weren't along?"

"I didn't say that."

"You didn't have to." Scott bent forward and passed a finger over the worried crease that lined Joanna's brow. "You'd better stop fretting. It'll make you look old before your time."

Joanna snickered. "That'd be appropriate, since I feel ancient."

Scott dropped his hand before he did something stupid. Like haul her into his arms and kiss her—kiss her until he'd erased that look of anguish and replaced it with one of dazed desire.

God, what was happening to him?

Forcing himself to draw back, he promised, "Tony and I will manage. You have my word on it. Don't even consider the possibility of failure."

"Unfortunately, that's not my style."

"Easier said than done, right?"

"When it comes to worrying, I could give a worry-wart warts."

Scott smiled. "So long as he doesn't give you wrinkles."

"What do you want to see next, Tony? The bears, the tigers? Or what about the elephants?"

"I don't care."

"Certainly you have a favorite animal."

"No."

"In that case, why don't we go to the nursery?"

"What's a nursery?"

Silently, Scott congratulated himself. Tony had actually asked a question. Only three words, but it was a quantum leap forward. When Scott had picked him up,

Tony had scarcely acknowledged his presence. In fact, Scott had had the uncomfortable feeling the boy was looking right through him.

"Haven't you ever heard the word *nursery* before?" Scott asked. Deliberately, he'd answered Tony's question with one of his own, a technique he urged on his teachers to get students to think for themselves rather than rely on being spoon-fed.

"I heard of nursery rhymes."

"What are they?"

"You don't know what nursery rhymes are?" The boy's eyes widened in disbelief. It was as if he were shocked to discover that he might possess a scrap of knowledge withheld from an adult.

Scott chuckled. "Sure, I do. I was just seeing how much *you* knew."

"My mom used to read 'em to me."

"Used to?"

"Yeah, she stopped when I wasn't a baby anymore."

"Is that right? So what does that tell you about nursery rhymes?"

All at once a light went on in Tony's eyes. "They're for babies."

"Then a *nursery* must be for—" Scott extended a hand, inviting Tony to finish the sentence.

"Babies."

"Right! Now do you know what we'll see when we go to the zoo nursery?"

"Babies!" Tony asserted.

"To be specific, baby animals."

"What kind?"

"That depends. Shall we check it out?"

"Okay."

Five minutes later, Tony pressed his face up against the glass partition separating the newborns and their "nurses" from the spectators. The antics of the small animals elicited much oohing and aahing from the crowd and, to Scott's delight, laughter from his side-kick.

"What kinda monkey is that?" The boy pointed a finger at a long-armed, reddish-brown primate being bottle-fed by a uniformed woman.

Scott read the sign attached to the top of the baby bed. "An orangutan."

"Where's his mom and dad?"

"I don't know."

"I think he'd like it lots better if his mom was feeding him."

"Perhaps she can't."

"Why not?"

"Oh, lots of reasons." Scott quickly scoured his mind for something plausible. "Maybe she's sick. Or maybe she had twins and didn't have enough milk for two."

Tony screwed up his face. "Or maybe she died."

Scott looked at the boy's image reflected in the glass partition. He seemed impassive, but Scott knew better. In a gentle voice he conceded, "That's a possibility."

"My dad died."

Scott slipped his hands into the back pockets of his jeans. He wasn't quite sure if he should pick up on Tony's remark or ignore it. The chance that he might be passing up an opportunity to diffuse some of the boy's animosity prompted him to say, "I know. Your mom told me."

Tony kept his eyes on the baby orangutan. "She did?"

"Uh-huh. I imagine you miss him a lot."

"I don't remember him very good. Mom says I was too little. But she has lots of pictures. She talks about him all the time."

The sliver of jealousy Scott experienced at the casual remark pricked his conscience. Reason told him he had no right to feel this kind of envy. But when it came to Joanna Parker, logic seemed to fly right out the window.

"I wish I had a dad," Tony suddenly confided. "Like other kids."

Scott's heart went out to the boy. "It would be nice if all children had both a mother and father. Unfortunately life's not always the way we'd like it. But that doesn't mean kids who have only one parent can't grow up to be healthy and happy. Take that little fellow." Scott indicated the orangutan still sucking greedily at his bottle. "I bet if we come back to the zoo next year, we'll find him out on the island with all the other monkeys, having himself a ball."

Tony turned serious eyes up at Scott. "You think so?"

"I know so." *And the same goes for you, Tony,* Scott added silently, taking the boy's hand. *By then, you're going to be enjoying life, too.*

He looked down at the small fingers enveloped by his and smiled. Wasn't this a start?

Chapter Four

If Joanna's living room weren't so small, Scott would have been pacing it like a caged tiger. As it was, he confined himself to an overstuffed chair. Digging his fingers into the arms of the recliner, he confessed, "I'm not sure if I'm frustrated, confused or irritated. I've tried every method I know, and I'm still not getting through to Tony."

Joanna set her cup on the coffee table. "Don't blame yourself, Scott. You've been wonderful. Nobody could have done more. Look at it this way—I haven't met with much better success, and I'm his mother."

"Failure never makes me feel good. Whether it's mine or somebody else's. Not that I think you've failed, but Tony isn't where either of us wants him to be. Not yet."

Joanna sighed. "I hate to suggest this, but perhaps I should contact Dr. Steiner. Maybe he could recommend a competent therapist in the area."

"I wish that weren't necessary, but we've about run out of options." Scott rubbed a hand along his jaw. "I don't like conceding defeat, but for the most part I've been batting zero with Tony."

Joanna crossed her legs and leaned forward. "If it's any consolation, he does seem better adjusted at home. He no longer sits alone in his room playing with Mike's chess pieces. Like right now. He's next door helping Kathy make fudge. Apparently my studying only after he's gone to bed has paid off."

"At what price?" Scott hadn't missed the dark smudges beneath her eyes. Though they were a sign that she could use more rest, he didn't find them unattractive. If anything, the shadowy underlining made her eyes seem positively huge. Touched by the cause as much as the effect, he gently chided, "You look worn out."

"That's not very complimentary."

"I didn't mean to sound judgmental. I was only making an observation. Please don't take offense. I already have my hands full with one hostile member of this household."

Smiling slightly, Joanna trained her gaze on her lap. "You're right, but I feel caught in the middle. I don't want Tony paying the price for my promotion. Yet now that I've committed myself, I have to follow through, and my job's demanding."

"Don't forget Tony'll reap the benefits from your hard work."

"And so will I," Joanna responded guiltily.

"Of course, and you deserve to. Give yourself that, Joanna. Even so, you can't keep burning the candle at both ends." He hesitated before adding softly, "Tony's not the only Parker I'm concerned about."

Joanna tried to dismiss the warmth in his voice. "That's kind of you, but I shouldn't have to put in too many more long nights. I've almost mastered the new data-base program."

"I'm glad."

"So am I. It's not easy going to bed at two and getting up at six."

"You've been operating on only four hours sleep a night? No wonder you're exhausted."

At his dark scowl, Joanna reminded him, "You dropped by to discuss Tony."

Scott slumped back in his chair, thinking that was only half the reason he was sitting in the Parker living room. The other was seated across from him. But he sensed Joanna wouldn't want to hear about that. "Right. You have any other questions?"

"After these outings Tony doesn't say much. Does he seem to be having any fun at all?"

"At times I could swear to it. Like last Sunday when I took him for the boat ride down the Delaware. At first he said no more than half a dozen words. Then he got caught up in watching the cityscape change and started asking all sorts of questions. Like which building was Independence Hall. And would we be able to see William Penn's statue on top of City Hall. I was impressed by how much he knew.''

''Before we moved, I picked up some guidebooks and told him a lot about Philadelphia. To spark his enthusiasm and kind of ease the transition.''

''He must have absorbed every word. Have you ever considered a career as a teacher?''

''Me, a teacher? I'm a little old to be going to back to college.''

''You didn't finish your degree?''

''No, I didn't.'' A sad smile crossed Joanna's face. ''Mike and I met during my freshman year and suddenly, getting my MRS was far more appealing than my BS. Since he was a senior and ready to graduate, neither of us fancied postponing marriage until I completed school. Originally I'd planned to take a few classes but decided to work instead so we could decorate our apartment in something other than Early Orange Crate. The next thing we knew, Mike's car fell apart and had to be replaced. One year became two, and two became three. When I was finally ready to register for my sophomore year, I found out Tony was on the way. Then Mike died and returning to college was out of the question.''

''I'm sorry.'' Not only did Scott regret the pain her memories had caused her, he lamented the jealous feelings any mention of her husband always aroused. More than eager to discuss something else, he said, ''But back to Tony. He was quite curious about Veterans Stadium.''

''Veterans Stadium?''

"I can see your study of Philadelphia didn't include local sports."

"I'm afraid not."

"Veterans Stadium is where the Phillies and Eagles play."

She angled her head innocently. "Phillies? Eagles?"

"Yeah. You know, the Phillies? Winner of the 1980 World Series? And the Eagles? NFL East champions in 1981?"

"The World Series, I'm familiar with. But the NFL?"

Scott chuckled. "You trying to pull my leg or something?"

"Or something?"

Suddenly the sparkle in her eyes was doing strange things to his insides. Reaching for his cooling cup of coffee, he observed, "We seem to have a knack for getting off the subject. As I was saying, Tony wanted to know about Veterans Stadium. Since—unlike his mother—he appears to be sports-minded, I thought I'd take him to the Eagles game next Sunday afternoon. If it's all right with you."

Joanna shook her head. "You're absolutely amazing."

"How's that?"

"I'd think by this time you'd be ready to give up on him."

"Well, I can't let Tony spoil my perfect record. I've always been a favorite of animals, children and old ladies."

And young ones, and middle-aged ones and adolescent ones, Joanna recounted mutely. Aloud she said, "If you want to give it another shot, it's okay by me."

Scott waited a beat, then proposed, "I think it'd be a good idea if you came along on these outings. Starting next Sunday."

Joanna looked startled by this sudden turn in the conversation. "I told you I'm not into sports—especially football. I only went in college because Mike was on the team. I worried he might get hurt and I wouldn't be there."

So Mike had been a big football hero! Scott's sole consolation was that Joanna had apparently been unimpressed. Flipping his hand, he observed, "That's not important."

"In other words, you don't care if I'm bored out of my mind?" Her smile took the edge off her words.

"Of course, I do, but... Look, I wouldn't have suggested it if I didn't think your participation would be good for Tony. From time to time I've picked up little hints that he feels guilty about leaving you home all alone."

"That's crazy. I've never given him... Are you serious?"

"Perfectly. He's let enough slip to convince me he feels bad about our going off without you."

"That's sweet." Joanna propped an elbow on the arm of the couch and braced her chin in a palm. After several contemplative minutes, she capitulated. "Okay, then, but I'll buy my own ticket. I won't have the One-for-One Club footing the bill."

"That won't be necessary. Since I'm the one asking, I'll be the one paying."

"Absolutely not. I insist."

He tossed her a crooked smile. "Why should you want to pay good money for the privilege of being bored to death?"

Joanna stood firm. "Anything for my son. Besides, mothers are used to making sacrifices. I'll purchase my own ticket, thank you. Otherwise, I won't go."

Scott shook his head and under his breath mumbled something about stubborn, independent women. To Joanna he announced, "I'll pick the two of you up next Sunday around twelve-thirty. Kickoff time is at two, but they always have some pregame activities lined up. By the way, I happen to know Lionel Holman. Maybe we can get his autograph for Tony."

"Lionel Holman?"

Scott's frown was suspicious. "You're not kidding around again, are you? I have a feeling you know more about football than you let on."

"No. Honest." She held up her hand as if swearing a solemn pledge.

"Lionel Holman's the Eagles starting quarterback. He's only twenty-five, but he's one of the highest paid players in the league."

"Where did you meet him?"

"He went to Whittier."

"Not while you were principal?"

"No, but his two younger sisters were students when I first came there, and he used to drop by to pick them up after school. Occasionally I'd run into him. He'd always ask me if the girls were keeping up with their studies. Lionel may be an athlete, but he doesn't minimize the importance of education.''

"I'm familiar with the type," she said, thinking of Mike. "And so now he's famous and making—what? Millions?''

"Yep. And it couldn't have happened to a nicer guy.''

"That's generous of you. Most people are jealous of highly paid athletes.''

"Don't think I'm not. I'm envious, all right. Envious as hell.''

"That's not the same as jealous.''

"Granted, but envy and jealousy are kissing cousins. Still, no amount of either can take away from what a great guy Lionel is.''

"I'll have to ask Tony if he's ever heard of him.''

"Do that. Just don't tell him we're going to ask for his autograph. I wouldn't want to disappoint him in case it doesn't work out." He pushed out of his chair. "I'd better be going. I have a meeting at six o'clock.''

From the hall closet Joanna retrieved Scott's trench coat and held it out to him. In the exchange, her hand brushed against his. Joanna flinched as if she'd touched a red-hot stove. Stepping back, she struggled to regain her equilibrium. "I—I can't thank you enough for what you've done . . . are doing for Tony.''

Scott pulled up his collar and turned to face her. "I wouldn't have it any other way. He's a terrific kid. All he needs is a nudge here and there to help him sort things out." Scott reached for the knob. "See you Sunday."

"Would you like some ice cream?" Scott asked.

Joanna groaned. "Absolutely not. I shot my junk-food allowance for the whole month in one afternoon."

"Tony, what about you? Think you could handle a Drumstick?"

"Could I, Mom?"

"You've already eaten enough to sink a ship."

"But I'm still hungry."

"Please don't whine," she admonished her son, though secretly she was pleased. In the last hour, he'd been making noises typical of a five-year-old.

Scott leaned toward Joanna. "Watching football takes lots of energy. Doesn't it, Tony?"

"Yeah."

"Okay, okay. How can I possibly stand up against the two of you?" She rummaged in her purse for her wallet, but before she could pull out some money, Scott had already handed a bill to his neighbor, who in turned was passing it on down to the teenager hawking ice cream in the stands.

Joanna tried to reimburse Scott, but he waved her off. "My treat."

"It's been your treat all day. And that wasn't our agreement."

"I'm an old-fashioned kind of guy. When I invite a lady out, I expect the date to be on me."

"This isn't a date."

"Isn't it?"

Joanna was saved a reply when at that moment an Eagles lineman intercepted a pass on the fifteen-yard line. As one, eighty thousand fans surged to their feet. So that Tony could see over the heads of those in front, Scott scooped the boy into his arms. Along with the rest of the crowd, they shouted as the burly defensive player twisted and turned, feinted and dodged his way up the field. When at last he plunged over the goal line for a touchdown, pandemonium broke loose.

"Wow, Mom. Did you see that?" Tony asked breathlessly as he slid down Scott's body and regained his seat.

"How could I miss it?"

He turned to Scott, "Who made the touchdown?"

"Nate Fields."

"What position does he play?"

"He's a nose tackle."

"A what?" Joanna put in.

"A nose tackle."

She sputtered with laughter. "What's his job? Tackling noses?"

Scott looked offended. "He tries to get to the opposing team's quarterback and take him out while he still has hold of the ball."

Joanna swiped at the tears rolling down her cheeks. "*Nose tackle*—how can grown men use such a term without cracking up?"

"Come on, Mom." Tony glanced around him as if ashamed of his mother's ignorance.

"Yeah, come on, Mom," Scott chimed in imitation. "Get with it."

Tony looked at Scott, his expression serious. "She doesn't know much about football."

"I sort of figured she didn't. Maybe we should teach her a few of the basics."

"Maybe *she*," Joanna inserted, "wouldn't care to learn."

Tony and Scott stared at her as if they couldn't believe what they'd heard. Joanna glanced from one to the other. "And I'd appreciate it if you wouldn't talk about me as if I were somewhere else. *She* indeed. It's disrespectful. Even if I'm not *with it*."

"Sorry, Mom."

"Yeah, sorry, Mom," Scott echoed.

Joanna glared at him. "Would you stop, already? I'm not your mother."

"For which I'm grateful," he returned smoothly. Before she had a chance to ponder his words, Scott pointed to the field. "Look there. Since the Eagles made the last touchdown, you'll see the ball being spotted for their kicker. Now this part is known as the kickoff. Of course, the object of the game—"

"I know what the object of the game is."

"Good—"

"I also know what the kickoff is."

"Good—"

"And a touchdown. I'm even aware of what a first down is," she said smugly. "Not to mention the fact that to gain yardage, the ball is carried on the ground . . . or thrown through the air."

"That's called a pass," Scott informed her, wondering if he dared throw one of his own. Directly at Joanna. "Is that the extent of your knowledge?"

"What else is important?"

"Lots," he said meaningfully, resting his arm along the back of Tony's seat. "You've only scratched the surface. Ever heard of sacking the quarterback? That's quite a move. Or how about the shotgun position?" He moved his hand deliberately until it came to rest on her shoulder.

Joanna stared at him, unblinking. They could have been the only two people in the world. Unable to form any words, she simply shook her head.

"You have a great deal to learn," he said huskily. "And I'm going to enjoy teaching you."

Joanna licked her lips. How could every nerve ending in her body be humming? Because, she warned herself, Scott Hartman had a more provocative game than football on his mind.

The magical spell was broken when the clock ticked off the final second and Eagles fans rose in unison to celebrate the score: Philadelphia 33, the opposing team 17. Lionel Holman, the undisputed star of the game for having thrown three touchdown passes, was carried off the field on the shoulders of his teammates.

"Well, Tony, how about the two of us going down to the locker room? Maybe we can get an autograph for you."

"You think we can?"

"We won't know unless we give it a try." Scott held out a hand. "Hang on tight. We don't want you getting lost in the crowd. And that goes for you, too," he said to Joanna, looping an arm around her waist.

Joanna could scarcely draw air into her lungs. Not because of the crush of the crowd but because of Scott's hand pulling her closer and closer until their bodies were practically melded together. Thigh against thigh, hip against hip. She was acutely aware of the stiff texture of his jeans, the softness of his shirt. His body heat seemed to be burning its way through her own clothing.

When they finally reached the bottom level of the stadium, her legs were about as capable of supporting her as wet noodles. Sitting down, she watched Scott and Tony disappear into the cavernous tunnel leading to the Eagles locker room and tried to pull herself together. After Mike's death she never expected to welcome a man's touch again.

But Scott was different. Simply being near him was enough to make her pulse quicken, her stomach flip. Could it be that two years of celibacy had finally caught up with her? Or, as she suspected, did her attraction to him involve more than mere physical appeal?

The thought frightened Joanna almost to the point of paralysis. Experience had taught her that it wasn't "better to have loved and lost than never to have loved at all." Losing Mike had nearly destroyed her.

"Hey, Mom, look at this," Tony shouted, his excitement pulling Joanna out of her reverie. He thrust into her hand a football card picturing the Eagles star quarterback.

"To Tony," she read. "Thanks for being a fan. Lionel Holman." She gave a pleased laugh. "So you did get his autograph."

"Mr. Hartman did. But Lionel Holman shook my hand."

"How nice! I hope you thanked Mr. Hartman."

"I forgot." Wide-eyed, Tony gazed up at Scott. "Thank you, Mr. Hartman."

Scott crouched down so their eyes were on a level. "Happy to oblige. I know how much an autograph like this would have meant to me at your age. That's why I brought the card along."

Out of the blue Tony threw his arms around Scott's neck and gave him a quick hug. Then, apparently embarrassed, he promptly stepped back and sought his mother's hand.

For a tense moment not one of the three spoke. It was Joanna who finally broke the silence. "What do you say we take Mr. Hartman out for a Big Mac."

"Yeah!"

"And—" she turned her gaze on Scott "—what says Mr. Hartman?"

Scott smiled broadly. "To tell you the truth, Mr. Hartman hates Big Macs. That's okay, though, since *he's* not around to object. And *I* happen to love them!"

Joanna laughed. "I wasn't talking about your father.... So is this a hint you'd like me to call you by your first name? Even," she whispered, "in front of little big ears?"

"How did you guess?"

"Do you think that's a good idea?" Uncertain, she looked down at Tony, but his puzzled expression indicated they might just as well be conducting their conversation in Swahili.

"Not good. Excellent." Scott lifted a hand to touch the tips of her shoulder-length hair. "Because, if I have my way, Tony's going to be seeing quite a lot of me, and he'd soon recognize the pretense."

Joanna's heart, which had nearly stopped beating, took off at a frantic gallop. In a thin voice, she remarked, "You still haven't answered my question."

"What question?"

"Will you let us buy you dinner?"

He flashed her an engaging grin. "I think I could be persuaded."

Chapter Five

One afternoon ten days later, Scott was tallying up some budget figures for that night's school board meeting when a light rap sounded at his door. In response to his "Come in," Tony poked his head around the frame.

"Mrs. Dexter said you wanted to see me."

"Yes, Tony." Scott rose and steered the boy to a corner of the office arranged for informal conversation.

"I—I didn't do anything bad," Tony spluttered as he scooted onto a chair.

"I know. I didn't call you here because you're in trouble. Quite the opposite. I think it's about time you returned to Mrs. Drummond's class."

The smile that spread across Tony's face was as broad as a jack-o'-lantern's—and about as jagged. Absently, Scott caught Tony's chin between his thumb and forefinger and rolled back his lower lip. "When did that happen?"

Tony stuck his tongue through a wide gap in his bottom teeth. "Last night. It's been loose about a week. I kept on wiggling it till it was hanging by this bloody stuff. Mom told me to stop. But I couldn't. It finally fell out."

"One more sign of how fast you're growing up. And since we're on the subject, I expect you to act like a big boy when you go back to Mrs. Drummond's room."

Tony's head bowed sheepishly. "I'm sorry I was bad."

"You weren't bad, sport, but you did some things that weren't nice." He patted the boy's knee. "However, it takes a real man to own up to his mistakes."

Tony's chest puffed out at the praise.

Scott toyed with a pencil. He avoided the boy's eyes while for long seconds he debated with himself. "Are we good enough friends for me to ask you something? It's kind of personal."

"I—I guess."

"Why did you misbehave when you first came to Whittier?"

Tony eyed Scott warily. "Promise you won't tell my mom?"

"Not if you don't want me to."

Tony heaved a heavy sigh. "I was mad 'cause we left my daddy."

Puzzled, Scott remarked, "I thought your father died before you moved here."

"He did. But before he went to heaven, Mom says he used to fix my toys and play ball with me. Stuff like that." The child's face clouded. "I don't remember any of that, though. You think it's okay—that I don't?"

Scott reached over and ruffled the boy's sandy hair. "It's only natural. You were very little when your dad went to heaven. That's why your mother tells you so much about him. She doesn't expect you to remember those things."

Tony didn't utter a word, but he visibly relaxed. Scott was getting the uncomfortable feeling that the five-year-old was somehow guilt-ridden because he had no direct memories of his father. Was Joanna unwittingly responsible for planting that idea in his head?

He didn't dwell overlong on the question because he still didn't have the answer he was seeking. "You say, Tony, that your father's in heaven, but you also told me you acted up in Mrs. Drummond's class because you left him in New York. I'm not sure I understand."

"Before we moved, we saw him all the time."

Summoning all his tact, Scott probed, "How did you see him?"

"I didn't mean we *saw* him. But we visited him in . . . in the cem—ceme—"

"Cemetery?" Scott completed for him, breathing an internal sigh of relief.

Tony nodded. "Mom always took flowers. We'd sit under a tree and she'd tell me stories about my dad. But then we came here. I didn't like us to move. Mom got so busy.''

"I see.'' The graveside visits, Scott reflected, had given Tony a needed sense of family. The child not only missed the shared closeness but also the extra measure of Joanna's attention he'd enjoyed before her new job put further demands on her time.

Tony turned soulful blue eyes on Scott. "She was home, but . . . we didn't do things.''

"You mean your mother didn't have time to play much with you,'' Scott remarked in an effort to clarify Tony's feelings. "Did you think you weren't important to her anymore?''

"Yes . . . no,'' Tony wavered.

"It can't be both. Tell me the truth, son.'' The intimate tag slipped out so naturally that Scott barely noticed it. "This is just between us men. Were you angry because your mother didn't seem to have much time for you?''

A sad expression marred Tony's small face, and Scott's heart melted at the softly murmured, "Yes.''

"Do you still feel that way?''

"Not no more. Now Mom doesn't get her books out until I'm in bed. And she's been going places with me.'' He grinned. "Like the football game. And she hates football.''

"In that case, maybe we ought to do something nice for your mom. What does she enjoy?''

Tony tipped his head at a thoughtful angle. "Umm, she likes flowers and trees and birds.''

"In other words, she's a nature freak.''

"I—I guess so," Tony reluctantly agreed.

At the boy's hesitance, Scott realized his error. To a five-year-old the word *freak* had to sound uncomplimentary. "I wasn't calling your mother a bad name. All I meant is that she likes getting outside and taking hikes in the woods."

"I don't know 'bout the woods. But she likes to go to the park. She says it's 'cause she grew up in the city with lots of cement."

"In that case, maybe we should plan a camping trip."

The sparkle in Tony's eyes spoke for him. "When?"

"How about after our game on Saturday? I'll have my camper loaded up, and we can take off for the rest of the weekend. You won't have to bring anything. I've got plenty of equipment for the three of us. And what I don't have, I can borrow." Scott paused an instant. "Should we tell your mother, or do you think we ought to keep our plans a secret?"

"Let's surprise her."

"Fine," Scott agreed with the boy, though for a slightly different reason. Recently Joanna had been putting up a fuss about their One-for-One trips taking up too much of his valuable time. Little did she realize that the most recent outings hadn't been official club activities at all, that he was acting on his own and picking up where One-for-One had left off. But Joanna didn't need to know that. Not just yet.

He smiled at Tony. "Shall we shake on it?"

Their hands joined in that timeless masculine ritual of making a pact.

"So it's a deal," Scott affirmed. "Tell you what. On Saturday, why don't you pack some pjs and a change of clothes for yourself. Just put them in the duffle bag you bring to the game. And don't forget underwear and a toothbrush."

"Okay! But what about Mom?"

Tony's gap-toothed smile squeezed at Scott's heart. The child was only five, but he wasn't thinking solely of himself. "Better throw in her toothbrush."

"And what she wears to bed?"

"Good idea." Scott tried not to picture Joanna in something black and lacy.

"I don't know what else."

"Let me worry about that." Scott was beginning to wonder if springing this trip on Joanna was such a good idea. He hadn't stopped to consider extra socks and jeans . . . not to mention panties and bras.

But he'd come up with something. No amount of hassle was too much if it put a genuine smile on Tony's face.

A surge of protectiveness shot through him. He wasn't certain when the need to make the boy feel secure in his new city and school had been transformed into a desire to take care of him. But there was no disputing that it had.

Nor could he deny that he wanted to do the same for Tony's mother.

"Who is this?" Joanna choked into the phone receiver.

"Let's just say I'm a taxpayer who's fed up with what's going on at Whittier. Why should I—and others like me—have to foot the bill so a special full-time aide can be hired to work with brats like your son?"

"But...but...I—"

"Believe me," the shrill voice on the other end of the line rudely interrupted, "I have every intention of getting petitions signed and taking them to the board. That pansy Hartman's doing nothing but wasting our money mollycoddling delinquents. Why should they have special privileges and classes? I say if they can't behave like decent, normal kids, then send 'em to reform school. And," the woman tacked on in an icy purr, "if that doesn't work, there are always more drastic measures!"

Before Joanna could get in a word, the receiver was slammed in her ear. A mixture of emotions raced through her. Outrage. Anger. Humiliation. But most of all fear. For one thing, she was afraid for Scott. The woman sounded bent on ruining his career. Even more, she was afraid for Tony.

All of a sudden Joanna began to shake uncontrollably. Making her way across the living room, she sank onto a chair and covered her face with her hands. Tears burned the backs of her lids. What should she do? Calling the police was out of the question. She couldn't give them any clues to the hectorer's identity, and even if she did lodge a complaint, what would that accomplish? The woman had simply made veiled threats, which, so far as Joanna knew, didn't constitute a crime.

When the doorbell chimed, she jerked upright and bounded out of her chair. It was past ten and she couldn't imagine who in the world was paying her a visit this time of night.

As she crossed to the door on unsteady legs, a frightening thought struck her. Suppose the woman on the phone was following up her call with a personal visit?

Joanna's heart hammered in her chest. Closing one eye, she glimpsed through the peephole. To her relief, she saw Scott standing on her doorstep.

"I know it's late," he said when she'd opened the door, "but the school board meeting just wound up. Before I headed home, I wanted to stop by and talk to you about Tony. Did he fill you in on our conver—" His smile fading, he lifted a palm to Joanna's cheek. "What's wrong? You look as if you've seen a ghost."

"Oh, Scott." The tears that had been threatening welled beneath her lids and blurred her vision.

Automatically, he stepped across the threshold and took her in his arms. "What is it, Joanna? Did something happen to Tony?" Against his shoulder he felt the shake of her head.

He released her just enough to nudge up her chin and look into her eyes. "What then? Why are you so upset?"

"I—I just had a frightening telephone call," she choked out.

"An obscene call?" Scott stiffened with anger.

"No, no, you don't understand," she protested. "It was a woman. An *angry* woman."

"What did she say?" Scott led Joanna to the couch and pulled a clean white handkerchief from his hip pocket. "I want every word. From the beginning."

Joanna blew her nose and waited for her nerves to settle. Drawing in a deep breath, she tried to keep her voice level. "About fifteen minutes ago when I answered the phone, this person...this woman started screaming at me. At first I thought she might be a drunk who'd dialed my number by mistake. But when she started talking about Tony, I knew the call was intended for me."

"She mentioned Tony? Why?" Scott's arm went around her shoulder in wordless encouragement.

Sniffing back her tears, Joanna explained, "She shouted that she was a taxpayer whose money was being squandered because Tony has a private school aide working with him. I got the impression she thought he was being favored."

Scott snorted. "Obviously the woman's not very perceptive. The kids in these programs don't see individual attention as a reward."

"She means to make trouble, Scott. Besides being upset about Tony, she threatened to circulate a petition to get you fired. Or words to that effect."

His eyes snapped in challenge. "Let her try."

"I don't think you should make light of this. It could be serious. She implied she wasn't beneath resorting to violence if she didn't get satisfaction. From the way she sounded, I swear the woman could be mentally unstable."

Scott's tone was dismissive. "I doubt it."

"But you didn't hear her, you didn't..." Joanna shuddered, unable to continue.

"Was there anything familiar about the voice?"

She hesitated before shaking her head. "No, nothing I can put a finger on."

"You sure? Try to think. If she knows about Tony, you may have met her."

"I—I can't pinpoint anything," Joanna said, though now that Scott mentioned it, there had been something that touched a responsive chord. But for the life of her she couldn't place it.

"I hate to ask this, but have you had any run-ins with your neighbors or colleagues?"

"No. Not a one." She dabbed the last trace of tears from her cheeks. "Things have gone smoothly at the office. And most people here in the apartment building are no more than acquaintances. Besides, between my job, housework and Tony, I haven't had time to make friends, let alone enemies."

"What puzzles me is why you were singled out. When it comes right down to it, our school helps plenty of children with problems. Tony's hardly the Lone Ranger." Scott's eyes narrowed in contemplation. "I wonder if any other parents have received threats."

"That would make more sense. And make me feel— if not exactly comfortable—at least not so alone. That's what's scary." She paused before speculating, "But what if they haven't?"

"Then we're back to—" he caught himself before saying *you* "—square one."

"But why should some woman want to get at me through Tony? What possible—" Abruptly, Joanna's mouth fell open as the memory of a woman's throaty purr came to mind. "Abby Wilson! I bet it was Abby Wilson who called!" she said with conviction.

"What makes you so positive?"

"The voice. It had a—a sort of feline quality."

Scott cocked an eyebrow. "Abby does strike me as the catty type."

"Perhaps, but that's not what I meant," Joanna qualified. Because she'd never confided in Scott about Abby's big plans to snare him, she chose her words carefully. "At the first soccer practice, I overheard Abby talking about a certain man."

"Probably her ex-husband. There's no love lost between the two."

"Not Stan. Someone she was interested in. When his name came up, her voice practically dripped honey."

"You picked up that tone tonight? But I thought your caller was vindictive."

"She was. Even so, her voice had that same predatory quality. Instead of being warm, though, it was cold."

"Umm-humm." Scott considered Joanna's observation. "Now that I think about it, Abby can inject that sultry note on a whim. But what could she have against you?"

"I'm not sure. I didn't even think she knew I existed. I was under the impression that Abby has eyes for only one person."

Scott drummed his fingers against his lips. "You said she named this man?"

"Yes."

"Well, out with it." When Joanna failed to respond, he coaxed, "Hey, I'm not a gossip monger, but I'd like to know. Abby Wilson is a notorious flirt. It's my civic duty to give the poor guy fair warning."

"That shouldn't be difficult." She touched a finger to his chest. "Abby's after you."

Scott threw back his head and laughed. "Why didn't you ever tell me about this?"

"I didn't want you to think...you know...that I was jealous."

His lips curved in a very male, very self-satisfied smile. "And are you? Jealous?"

"I don't like the woman," Joanna countered, irked that he seemed so pleased with himself.

Scott rested a hand on her shoulder. "Neither do I. This may sound egotistical, but I knew Abby was trying to come on to me. She's about as subtle as a hooker. I've tried to be tactful, but after tonight I'm finished handling her with kid gloves."

"Don't do anything rash, Scott. What if I'm wrong? What if it wasn't Abby on the phone? It doesn't make sense that she'd take her anger out on me if she has it in for you."

"Doesn't it? 'Hell hath no fury like a woman scorned,'" Scott quoted, "especially when she sees the man has his eye on someone else."

Someone else. The words sent a stab of pain through Joanna's heart. "I had no idea you—you . . . were involved with somebody."

"Nothing's definite. But I'm working on it."

Why Scott's confession should disturb her, Joanna couldn't say. She wasn't interested in another relationship, but, nevertheless, she felt betrayed. On a deep breath, she protested, "Then I'd say you were spending too much time with Tony and me. You should be seeing more of your . . . lady friend."

"I'd like that. Are you willing to cooperate?"

"Why wouldn't I be?" she said stiffly. "I just said as much, didn't I?"

His fingers began to trace slow circles on her bare arm. "Don't you get it, Joanna? Can't you see what's obvious to Abby and everyone else? You're the woman I care about. You're the one I want."

Joanna licked her lips and tried once more to locate her voice. "Me?" she whispered huskily.

"Yes, you. I was lost the instant you walked through my office door."

Before Joanna had a chance to respond, Scott lowered his head and claimed her mouth. Though the kiss was soft and incredibly gentle, it kindled a warmth within her, a warmth she'd thought never to experience again. She felt at once comforted and excited. Until that moment, she hadn't realized how much she'd missed the touch of a man's lips, the feel of his arms holding her tight, the warmth of his body molded to hers.

Without thinking, she circled her hands around Scott's neck and kissed him back. She let her fingers wander into the hair at the back of his neck and reveled in its silkiness. The play of his mouth over hers, the soft wool of his pullover against her arms, the spicy scent of his after-shave—everything about him excited her. When one of his hands slipped to the base of her spine and pressed her even closer, a soft moan escaped her lips.

Encouraged by her response, Scott lifted his mouth to trail kisses along her jawline and over her slender throat. He felt her erratic pulse beating against his lips, her soft hands sliding down his arms and creeping around his waist. He'd fantasized about this moment for weeks, kissing her until he felt her body go limp, watching her eyes until they darkened with desire.

She felt so right in his arms that if he weren't careful, he'd lose control. *Slow, easy,* he cautioned himself. He wanted more than a few gentle caresses. He longed to strip her naked and make love to her then and there. But reason told him that she wasn't ready for that.

Reluctantly Scott released his hold, but he couldn't bring himself to let Joanna go completely. He brought his mouth to her ear and gave the lobe a playful nip. Sighing raggedly, he murmured, "I didn't come here intending for this to happen."

One part of Joanna yearned to stay within Scott's protective embrace. His beard-stubbled jaw moving against her own soft flesh was incredibly arousing, as was his moist breath whispering over her cheek. She had a crazy desire to run her hands over his finely honed body, learn its hard planes and muscular ridges, feel his skin quiver beneath her exploring fingertips. With a surge of panic, she realized how easy it would be to surrender to her emotions, to give her heart to Scott. But she couldn't allow that to happen. Loving and losing was too painful. It would be far better never to become involved in the first place.

And so, despite the strength of her desire, despite the craving of her body for his, the more cautious part of Joanna had her pushing away.

Fighting to regain her composure, she acknowledged, "No, I don't suppose you did. And it mustn't happen again."

"Why not?" Scott countered. "You aren't going to pretend you're not attracted to me, are you? After the way you just responded?"

Blushing, she lowered her eyes. "That isn't the point. You must understand, Scott. I'm just getting back on an even keel. I can't risk having my life turned upside down a second time. Not by you. Not by any man." Her voice caught. "I—I just can't."

"So instead you take the coward's way out—hang on to your husband's memory rather than chance another relationship. Is that it?"

"Whatever gave you that idea?"

"Tony says you're always looking at Mike's pictures, talking about him. I thought you were trying to help Tony remember his father, but now I'm not sure. I think you're doing it more for yourself."

"Don't try to second guess me! You have no right."

"We're not talking about rights here," Scott returned smoothly. "I'm speaking as a friend. It's not healthy to dwell on the past. You need to let Mike go—if not for your own sake, then for your son's."

"Let me remind you that Tony is my responsibility. *Mine*," she repeated for emphasis. "And it's *my* life you're talking about. I'll lead it any way I see fit."

"I'll not pressure you, Joanna. But at the same time, I won't let you shove me around. Like it or not, I'm in your life now. Yours and Tony's. And I intend to stay."

Joanna couldn't find the words to express her anger. Just who did Scott Hartman think he was, anyhow?

Her chin soared upward. "We'll see about that!"

"Count on it!" With lightning swiftness, he pulled her into his arms, trapping her hands between them and overpowering her mouth. His lips rocked over hers with bruising determination, robbing her of breath and reason. Joanna felt her knees buckle, her legs give way. She clutched at the wool of his sweater for support.

Then, as abruptly as it had begun, the kiss ended. With unaccustomed roughness, Scott thrust her from him. He was out the door almost before her dazed senses comprehended that he had left.

"Come on, guys!"
"Take the ball away from 'em!"
"Let's get a goal!"

At least thirty parents were on their feet, cheering the Tornadoes on in their last game of the season.

After a storm the night before had dumped nearly two inches of rain in less than an hour, Joanna had expected the match to be cancelled. But it was held anyway—on a muddy field.

Scott had insisted the kids would love the wet playing conditions. And he'd been right; the dirtier they got, the more they seemed to enjoy themselves.

Now, well into the fourth quarter, not one number on the back of a single uniform was readable.

The Tornadoes' record stood at oh and five. More by accident than design, Joanna surmised as her voice merged with the shouts of the other parents. All season they'd seemed to be the hard-luck team in their league. While those they'd played had managed to score by means of one fluke or another, the Tornadoes' forwards always missed the goal—by inches. This game was proving no different, except that the Rockets had also failed to score.

With only minutes left before the final whistle, it was impossible to tell who had control of the ball. Being so young, the players hadn't yet learned that in order to pass, they needed to keep some distance between them. Instead, it appeared that those on the field—regardless of their assigned positions—were chasing down the ball like starving dogs after table scraps.

Then, all of a sudden, one of the contestants broke from the pack, his short legs alternately pumping and dribbling the ball before him as he raced toward the Rockets' cage. Despite the filthy uniform, Joanna had no trouble identifying the player.

"That's it, Tony!" she yelled. "Keep control. Take it on in!"

On her last shout of encouragement, the ball sailed past the outstretched hands of the goalie and into the net. The Tornadoes went berserk—leaping into the air, clapping hands, slapping backs, clasping shoulders.

And the din! Joanna thought she must be back in Veterans Stadium!

Not five seconds after Tony's spectacular kick, the referee was blowing his whistle to signal the end of the game. Parents flooded onto the field to offer sons and daughters their hearty congratulations.

Joanna tried but found it impossible to get to Tony, whose teammates had dragged him into the largest puddle on the field. As if guided by some unwritten law of childhood, they started kicking and splashing water on one another. It wasn't too different, Joanna thought, from popping champagne bottles in the victor's locker room. For the next several minutes bedlam reigned until finally Scott put an end to the mayhem by calling the team together for a final pep talk.

"I want to tell you what a super job all of you did this morning—and the entire season," he praised as they gathered round. "Even when you were losing, you didn't give up but played your best. And while the record book may say we won only today's game, thanks to Tony—" he gave the boy a wink "—in my opinion, we won them all. You know why? Because you kids have the right spirit. And spirit's what counts. Thanks for coming out and playing. I hope to see you all back next September.''

En masse, the team let out an enormous whoop. Afterward the parents trooped by to thank Scott for his time and efforts with their children. Joanna watched as one by one they gave his hand a sincere shake. With a single exception. Abby Wilson. Her mumbled thanks was barely audible, the look on her face decidedly sour.

Joanna had received no more threatening phone calls, nor had she heard of any petition circulating about Scott, so he'd apparently taken care of Abby. Though curious about what he had said, she acknowledged that it was none of her affair.

After their heated kiss a few nights before, Joanna hadn't spoken to Scott. She was painfully embarrassed by her behavior and so held back as long as she could. With Tony securely at her side, she brought up the end of the line, wondering if Scott bore her a grudge. But when she extended her hand, he tucked it in the crook of his arm. The easy greeting seemed to deny that she'd ever raised her voice to him in anger.

"Ready to get out of here, Pele?" Scott asked pleasantly.

The boy turned his mud-streaked face up at Scott. "You bet!"

The sparkle of anticipation in her son's eyes hinted that something was up between the two of them. But what, Joanna had no idea. Unsuccessfully she tugged at her imprisoned hand. "You both look as pleased as canary-swallowing cats. And as mysterious as sphinxes. What's up?"

"It's a secret," Scott informed her.

"And a surprise!" Tony added.

Scott threaded his fingers through Joanna's. "I have to stop off at my place, but I shouldn't be more than an hour. That ought to give Tony plenty of time to get cleaned up."

"For what?" Joanna persisted.

"We're taking you for a little ride."

In spite of herself, she laughed. "You sound suspiciously like a hit man for the mob."

"Are we enemies?" Scott asked, his voice low. When Joanna didn't answer, he said, "Trust me. This is one trip you're going to enjoy."

"Maybe I should pass. You and Tony go alone."

Tony's face fell. "No, Mom. We're gonna have fun. You can't not go."

Joanna sighed resignedly. How could she dampen her son's excitement? He was enjoying an unaccustomed high, especially after he'd led his team to their sole victory of the season. She'd have to put her personal feelings about Scott aside.

Giving Tony's smudged cheek a gentle caress, she surrendered. "Okay, okay."

"I knew you wouldn't let us down," Scott affirmed.

As they strolled toward their cars, Joanna asked over her shoulder, ''What should I wear?''

''You're fine as you are.'' More than fine, he thought to himself, giving the close-fitting knit top and jeans a lazy inspection.

Chapter Six

Less than an hour later, the trio—plus Miss Kitty—were cruising along the Pennsylvania Turnpike, headed toward Reading.

For the past ten miles a puzzled frown had creased Joanna's forehead. "Tell me where you're taking me, Hartman," she finally demanded. "If you don't, I'll have you arrested for kidnapping."

Scott took his eyes from the road long enough to give her a thorough masculine appraisal. "I hate to be the one to break the news, but you ain't no kid."

Joanna squirmed in the bucket seat, discomfited both by his appreciative survey and the hint of suggestion in his voice. Defensively, she arched her neck. "Tony is."

"That won't wash. He's in on the plot."

"Just what conspiracy have you two cooked up?"

"Another half hour and you'll know."

Joanna folded her arms over her chest and scooted down into the seat. For a time she concentrated on the gently rolling countryside. Surprisingly, after the terrible storm the night before, it had turned out to be a glorious October day, with the afternoon temperature hovering in the mid-seventies. The leaves were beginning to change, and their warm reds, oranges and yellows provided a magnificent contrast to the cool blue sky.

Before long, Joanna's eyelids began to droop. The sun's bright rays filtering through the windshield had practically lulled her to sleep when Tony's excited "Look, Mom!" snapped her to attention.

"W-what?" she responded automatically.

"Over there. Three deer! Did you see them run into the trees?"

"Sorry, honey, but they were too quick for me."

Tony's disappointment showed on his face.

"Don't worry, Tony," Scott put in. "There are lots of deer around. With any luck at all, we should spot more this weekend."

Joanna's ears pricked up. "Weekend?"

"Uh-oh." Scott glanced over his shoulder at Tony, his expression apologetic. "I think I let the cat out of the bag."

Tony's eyebrows rose inquiringly. "You keep Miss Kitty in a bag?"

Scott chuckled. "To 'let the cat out of the bag' means I said something I shouldn't have."

"Why couldn't you say so? Why did you talk about cats?"

"Good question." Amused, Scott tried to come up with a definition of figurative language the boy could understand. "That's how people talk sometimes—in a roundabout way."

"They do? Why?"

Scott was still trying to explain himself a half hour later as they took the exit marked Tomaqua State Park.

Within minutes Scott was expertly wheeling into the spot assigned them by the park ranger.

"But what if I have other things to do this week-end?" Joanna protested, noting that only a handful of campers seemed to be taking advantage of the park that particular Saturday.

"What could be more important than spending to-day and tomorrow in the great outdoors? We're not going to get much more weather like this, you know. Before we turn around, the snowflakes'll be flying."

"Granted, but—"

"Tony and I had a long talk, and he assured me you didn't have a hot date for tonight—"

"A hot date!"

Scott put the van in neutral, set the brake and cut the engine. "You don't, do you?"

"I'm not looking for a relationship. Ergo, I don't date."

"So, what's the problem?"

Joanna jabbed a finger at him. "First off, whether or not I had plans for tonight is moot. Social engagements may not be one of my priorities, but I don't exactly vegetate on weekends. There're dozens of things claiming my time—cleaning, grocery shopping, washing, mending. And here you drag me off into—" Joanna looked around her "—the wilderness."

"None of that sounds like a national emergency. Anyhow, I'll have you home tomorrow in time for the essentials. So relax." Scott gave her his most engaging smile. "And one more thing—I haven't hauled you into the wilderness. Walk down that path about a hundred yards and you'll find all the comforts of home—showers, with both hot and cold running water, washers, dryers. You name it and Tomaqua State Park has it."

"What about food?"

Without answering her, he said to Tony, "Roll back that blanket, will you, sport?" When the boy had done as he was instructed, Scott pointed out, "See? A picnic basket. A cooler. You could put together a veritable gourmet dinner with everything I packed."

Joanna wasn't about to be mollified. "How about those other little amenities called toothbrush, toothpaste, pajamas...*underwear*." She drew out the last word for special emphasis.

"Not to worry. Tony and I have it all arranged. He threw some things into his duffel bag, didn't you, Pele?" The look of horror on the boy's face told Scott he hadn't.

"I—I forgot," he stammered. "Mine and Mom's."

"Hey, no problem," Scott assured in an effort to stem the tears that had sprung to the little fellow's eyes.

"No problem!" Joanna complained. "I'm out here in the middle of nowhere without even the most basic trappings of civilization, and all the man can say is 'no problem.'"

Scott waved a thumb over his shoulder. "Up the road a mile or two, there's this grocery. More than a grocery, actually. It carries jeans, socks, shirts. After supper, I'll drive you there, and you can stock up on whatever you need."

"We don't *need* anything. I just went into hock outfitting Tony for school. My credit card has been stretched to the limit."

"Don't get so uptight. This was all my idea, so I'll foot the bill for whatever—"

"I wouldn't hear of it," she cut in.

"What choice do you have? Unless you want to live in your clothes for two days. Maybe you can, but I doubt Tony'll make it. Kids can get pretty grubby in short order." He turned toward Tony, a clear indication that he'd entertain no arguments. "In the meantime, fella, I think there's enough of the afternoon left for you and me to catch our supper."

"What're we gonna eat?" Tony asked suspiciously, not exactly certain what Scott had in mind by the word *catch*.

"Fish, naturally."

"Wow! I never been fishin'!"

"If we hike in that direction—" Scott indicated the trail to their right "—we'll run into the prettiest, clearest little stream. Best trout fishing in the world."

"And what am I supposed to do while the two of you are off playing Daniel Boone?" Joanna asked.

Scott compressed his lips thoughtfully. "Watch?"

"How thrilling."

"Or if you're of a mind, you can try your luck. I brought along three poles."

"Terrific! I can be bored . . . or extremely bored."

Scott laughed. "Come on, city girl. Afraid you might find out you enjoy country living?" He bounded out of the van and opened the rear doors to retrieve the fishing gear. Tony was right on his heels.

"Fat chance," Joanna grumbled when at last she climbed down and joined them.

"Here, you can carry this." Scott thrust the tackle box into her hands.

"What about Miss Kitty?" Tony inquired.

"We'll take her along." Scott slammed the doors shut, turned the key in the lock and set off on the path through the woods. Tony was only a few feet behind, with Joanna bringing up the rear. A rather distant rear. Her mood wasn't improved when she stubbed her toe on an exposed tree root. She should have stayed in the van, she kept telling herself as she trudged on, following the two fleet-footed figures moving in front of her.

After what seemed to Joanna an eternity, the path finally widened on the rim of a clearing above a rocky, slow-moving stream.

"Let's get a move on," Scott urged.

When they were close to the water's edge, Joanna set the tackle box at his feet. In an instant he was rummaging through it, attaching lures to the lines on each pole. "You can put Miss Kitty down, Tony. She won't run off—not when she gets her catnip to play with." Scott located a small crocheted mouse, and the cat pounced on the toy with all the enthusiasm of a drunk offered a shot of whiskey. Then Scott handed one of the poles to Tony. "Take this down to the stream, but don't try anything with it yet. I'll show you how to cast. Ditto for you, Jo."

Joanna's heart gave a little lurch. Never in her life had she allowed anyone to shorten her name—not even Mike. She'd always thought the diminutive too masculine, but sliding off Scott's tongue, it sounded soft and smooth and decidedly feminine. Retreating into a pleased silence, she took the pole and followed Scott along the bank.

"Now, watch this," he instructed. "I'm aiming for that big boulder." After making sure that the line was reeled in completely, he moved his arm back and forth, much like a baseball player taking a few practice swings before stepping into the batter's box. Slowly, he brought the rod back, then forward. When it reached the top of his shoulder, he flicked his wrist and with a hiss the leader sailed upstream, landing in a shallow pool alongside the rock.

Tony's eyes rounded. "Wow! Can I try that?"

"Sure. Will you hold this, please?" Scott gave his rod to Joanna and went down on a knee. With one large hand covering the boy's, he went through the motions of casting.

When the lure dropped into the water scant inches from Scott's, Tony jumped up and down, shouting, "I did it, I did it!"

"And on your first try, too," Scott commended.

"When do I catch a fish?"

"You have to wait until one bites."

"How long's that?"

"Can't tell. Sometimes it's a matter of minutes. Sometimes hours."

"Hours!"

Scott gave him an encouraging pat. "Maybe. Maybe not. But if you want to fish, you have to be patient."

"Was it fishing that taught you patience?" Joanna asked.

Scott faltered before answering. "Among other things."

Joanna frowned, puzzled by the odd catch in his voice. But before she had an opportunity to mull it over, he was insisting, "Time for your lesson."

"I think I'd prefer being a spectator."

"That's no fun." He took his rod from her and quickly reeled in the line. After leading her downstream a few yards, he showed her how to cast—just as he had Tony—but with one major difference. He snaked his left arm around her waist and pulled her against him. With her back plastered to his front, Joanna almost forgot to breathe.

"It's all in the wrist," he murmured, closing her fingers about the handle. His voice feathered her ear with its husky whisper, raising goose bumps along every inch of her skin.

Scott demonstrated the motion by wrapping his own hand around hers and flicking his wrist several times. "Feel that action?"

Joanna felt the action all right, from her neck to her ankles. Every spot where their bodies touched seemed to have taken on a life of its own. "I think so," she managed to get out, though her voice had a raspy quality.

"Okay. Let's aim for that spot right over there." Against her temple she felt his nod accompany the direction of his hand toward a willow on the stream's bank. "Easy does it," he cautioned, pulling the tip back and then snapping it forward. When the lure fell short of its destination by several feet, he remarked, "Looks like we'll have to try again. We won't give up until we get it right."

While she cranked the reel, Scott's thumb unerringly found a gap between her top and jeans and began a slow rotation along the exposed flesh.

Joanna tensed. It was as if her every nerve had been tightly wired. She could feel the solid wall of his chest rising and falling against her back, feel the callused pad of his thumb tracing fiery circles beneath her rib cage, feel the light touch of his lips feathering over her hair.

When at length his hand slid under the stretchy fabric of her top and crept upward in ever widening circles, Joanna tried to form an objection, but she couldn't. A liquid warmth surged through her, leaving her too weak for speech.

Reflexively she matched her own turns on the reel with the movement of his hand. Her mind clouded by a sensuous haze, Joanna let her head fall back against his shoulder and her eyelids flutter shut.

Scott's fingers found her breast, and he paused to knead softly. At her tiny moan of pleasure, his thumb flicked once, then twice over her nipple, bringing the sensitive tip to a turgid peak. "God, I want you," he rasped, his moist breath dampening the shell of her ear. His left arm drew her yet closer as he ground his hips against her backside and wedged the hardened flesh into the base of her spine.

"I—I . . . want . . ."

"Want what, sweetheart?"

His left hand had joined his right under her sweater and was lavishing loving attention on her other breast.

"I—I want you to stop."

"No you don't."

"But Tony—"

"Is preoccupied. And with our backs to him, he can't see a thing."

"Please, Scott. My knees feel like Jell-o."

"Mine, too. I just wish we were alone."

One hand moved downward and maneuvered beneath the waistband of her jeans. When his fingers fanned possessively over her belly without so much as a hint of denial from her, she realized she was lucky to have a five-year-old chaperon.

"Coach Hartman! I've got one!" Tony screamed at the top of his lungs.

Had the parents of Scott's students heard his harsh expletive, it would have raised more than a few eyebrows. In a fraction of a second, he was racing back upstream toward Tony. On rubbery legs Joanna followed.

"Hang on to it," Scott directed the boy as he bent beside him.

"I need help."

"No you don't. Just start to reel him in. Slowly, carefully. And you'll have him right where you want him." The words were directed at Tony, but Scott's eyes were on Joanna.

Flustered by his penetrating gaze, she dropped her own to the ground and tried to concentrate on Scott's directions to her son. But she couldn't. Her body still tingled from the sensation of his sure hands roaming over her bare skin.

With the memory came longing. And fear. Where Scott was concerned, she was in danger of breaking her vow to never again lose her heart. If she wasn't careful, she'd soon find herself hopelessly bound to him.

With an effort Joanna lifted her eyes and focused on the scene before her. Tony had just pulled in a fish that was about four inches long.

"Can we have him for supper?" Tony asked.

"I'm afraid not," Scott responded. "He's not a keeper."

"What's a keeper?"

"A fish that's large enough to eat. Judging by the length, this one's hardly out of diapers."

Tony's eyes widened. "I didn't know fish wore diapers."

What started as a chuckle turned into a full-fledged roar. "We're going to have to do something about that literal mind of yours."

Tony seemed unperturbed. "Can I cast again?"

"By all means." Scott released the fish back into the water. "Want some help?"

"Nope. I'll do it myself."

Scott stood erect, pleased that the boy wasn't deflated over the loss of his first catch.

Tony thrust his tongue out in concentration as he drew the rod over his shoulder, then let it fly. Instead of landing in the pool beside the boulder, his line wrapped around a tree limb.

"Uh-oh. I goofed."

"Goes with the territory." Quickly, Scott slipped off his shoes and socks and waded into the stream. In a matter of seconds he'd untangled the nylon cord and was encouraging Tony to try again. This time the lure fell several yards short of the spot he was aiming for.

"Give it another shot," Scott coaxed. He was about to add *third time's the charm,* but thought better of it. He wasn't up to further interrogation from the inquisitive five-year-old.

Once more Tony duplicated the motion. Accidental or not, the line plopped right next to the boulder.

"Super job, Tony. Maybe this is the spot where you'll haul in that big one for supper."

A lump formed in Joanna's throat at the easy camaraderie that existed between the two. Before Scott had come into their lives, she hadn't realized just how starved for male companionship Tony had been. But as she watched, she regretted her blindness. As good a mother as she was, she couldn't provide her child with all the things a boy should have. Even though she convinced herself she didn't truly want Scott, she knew Tony needed him.

As the sun sank in the west, Scott stirred the coals of their campfire. "Can I get you anything else?" he asked Joanna, who sat on one of the folding lawn chairs he'd supplied.

She patted her stomach. "No thanks. Another bite and I'll burst. That was some spread you put on, Mr. Hartman."

"I told you we were in for a gourmet's delight."

"I'm not sure hot dogs and hamburgers qualify as elite fare, but they did taste wonderful."

"Food eaten outdoors always does."

Joanna picked up her glass of lemonade. "I can't argue with that."

"I know Tony was disappointed we couldn't keep either of the fish he caught, but maybe next time."

"Perhaps," she said aloud. *If there is a next time.* "At any rate, catching those small fish was a big thrill for him. Thanks for giving him the chance. Many men would have sent him packing after he got that line so tangled up, but you...you're so patient. I'm surprised you haven't ever..." Her words trailed off.

"Surprised that I haven't ever what?"

Joanna shrugged. "You know...married. And had a dozen kids of your own. You're really good with them."

"I was married," he corrected, his voice a bit distant.

"Y-you were?" Joanna stammered, startled by the admission.

"For five years."

At the same time she was telling herself it was none of her business, she was asking, "Were you divorced?"

"Several years ago."

"I'm sorry," Joanna said.

"At first I was, too." Scott, who'd been standing, took a seat in the other lawn chair, debating whether or not to get into his past. Finally he decided there was no time like the present. If, as he intended, Joanna was to become a part of his future, she deserved to know about his ex-wife.

He stretched out his long frame and linked his fingers, the gesture pensive. "We didn't see eye to eye about what was important in life. Emily wanted money, power, prestige. I wanted friends, family... children."

"How did two people with such different outlooks get together in the first place?"

"Don't think I haven't asked myself that same question a thousand times. I never pretended to care about the almighty dollar. Whenever I look back on it, I wonder why Emily ever married me."

Joanna could think of any number of reasons why a woman would consider Scott good husband material, but she wasn't about to enumerate them. Instead, she said nothing, her silence encouraging him to go on.

"I think sometimes it was because of her background." Scott leaned over and again stirred the fire. "She was the oldest of six children. Her father was a coal miner, and they never had two nickels to rub together while she was growing up."

When Scott volunteered nothing more, Joanna prompted, "Where did you meet?"

"At college. Emily had a full scholarship. With that, and two jobs, she managed to get through school." He looked at Joanna, who was hugging the tops of her arms. "Cold?"

"A bit."

Scott went to the van, where Tony was playing with Miss Kitty, and retrieved a lightweight jacket. Joanna bent forward and he slipped it around her shoulders. She wanted to hear more about his failed marriage, not out of a morbid sense of curiosity but from a desire to know him better. She didn't stop to ask herself why that was. She simply accepted it.

Once he was again settled in his chair, he picked up where he'd left off. "The first two years of our marriage couldn't have been better. Then the trouble began. Initially it was a subtle change in attitude—Emily's wanting a little bigger house, a little better car. I told her both were fine with me, since it was time we started a family."

He stared into the fire. "In the beginning she didn't come right out and say she didn't want children. She claimed she wasn't quite ready. I was disappointed, but I told myself to give her time. That she'd come around.

"Then Emily started pushing me to get a better-paying job. This time her hints weren't so veiled. We started fighting. I was perfectly content being a grade-school principal, but she was far more ambitious. Emily thought with my background in administration I should take a job with industry." His tone was wry. "Industry, as you know, pays a hell of a lot more than education."

He paused. "The morning of our fourth anniversary, we were at the breakfast table when I took a long, hard look at my wife and thought, 'You're living with a stranger.' But I couldn't bring myself to end it. She did that. We started going our separate ways. To be honest, I didn't mind coming home to an empty house. At least that way I got some peace. I figured Emily was shopping or running errands, but instead she was out looking for a better prospect. When she found him, she told me she'd filed for divorce."

Joanna was tempted to reach out and smooth the lines on Scott's forehead, but she didn't dare. "That must have been a terrible blow."

"Not to my heart. By that point, whatever had been between us was dead. But my male pride did take a battering. At first I wanted to get even by giving Emily all kinds of grief about the divorce. I'm embarrassed to say that I agreed not to contest it if I got the house, the car, the savings account—the works. She could have her clothes and personal possessions. Naturally, she threw a fit. After a while I got tired of fighting. I wanted out, too. So I quit playing the bastard and we came to a mutually agreeable settlement."

Scott propped an ankle on his knee. "As it turns out, I was a fool to have taken her rejection personally. I lasted longer than any of the others have." At Joanna's questioning frown, he explained, "Emily's on her third husband now, and I wouldn't be surprised if number four isn't waiting in the wings. In a way, it's very sad. Each has had considerably more wealth than the other, but I don't suppose any man will ever have enough for her. I've often thought if Emily had had more when she was growing up, maybe she wouldn't have become so greedy."

"Perhaps," Joanna inserted. "Perhaps not. Maybe that's her nature."

Scott shrugged. "Could be."

"You don't seem to have suffered any permanent scars."

"True. I had to force myself to get on with my life. It's the only way to deal with disappointment and trauma."

Joanna squirmed uncomfortably, wishing she'd kept quiet. The penetrating gaze Scott turned on her said it was time she put her own past behind her.

"Well, I suppose I'd better be getting Tony ready for bed," Joanna said, rising. Without another word, she headed for the van.

Only after threatening her son with a spanking was she able to separate him from Miss Kitty and escort him to the bathhouse for a shower.

While they were gone, Scott made quick work of transforming the back seat into a double bed. He'd finished rolling his sleeping bag out near the fire when Tony and Joanna returned to the campsite.

Watching them approach brought a spontaneous grin to his face. Tony was in the pajamas they'd picked up at the store down the road. The smallest pair they could find were about three sizes too large. The boy had rolled up the legs to avoid tripping on the excess material and was clutching a handful of elastic waistband to keep the pants from falling down.

"Come here, sport," Scott said, producing a large safety pin from a round metal container that had once held Christmas cookies. "This'll fix you up."

Joanna climbed into the van behind her son. Reaching for nonchalance but falling short, she said, "I think I'll take my turn with soap and water in the morning. Good night, Scott."

Before she could make good her escape, he locked a hand around her arm. "It's only nine-thirty," he observed in a quiet voice.

"I know, but it's been an exhausting day. An exhausting week."

"In that case," he said, releasing her but letting his fingers trail down the bare skin, "sleep well."

Chapter Seven

"Here's Sir Guy on his magnificent charger, galloping at top speed, his lance thrust out in front of him. Whumph! He hits Sir Hugh with all the force of a cannonball. In a flash they're off their steeds, each drawing a sword. 'Take that, Sir Hugh!' Guy shouts."

A single thrust of Scott's imaginary weapon sent a head of iceberg lettuce skittering across the kitchen counter and onto the floor.

"Yay!" Tony cheered. "Sir Guy chopped his head off!"

Joanna, who'd been standing in the doorway, watching the make-believe joust, decided it was time to intercede. Hands parked on hips, she marched into the kitchen. "What in heaven's name is going on here?"

Tony spun around on a heel, his face reddening. "We were only having a little fun."

"Do tell!" Joanna looked from her son directly at Scott. "I thought I left you in charge of tearing up greens for a salad."

"Uh, that's what we were doing. Right, partner?"

Tony gave a brisk bob of his head. "Right!"

"*Butchering* my lettuce is more like it." Joanna bent to pick up the bedraggled head and set it back on the counter. "At least you have the good grace to look ashamed of yourself, Hartman."

"It'll never happen again, sir...ma'am." Scott clicked his heels and gave her a mock salute.

Joanna fought off a smile. "See that it doesn't, Private," she returned in her best drill-sergeant imitation.

"Rats!" Tony complained. "Just when it was my turn."

"In the future, young man, I suggest you confine any medieval battles to your chess pieces." She turned around, then swung back to them. "Come to think of it, why don't you learn to play the game. That would certainly put those knights and kings to better use."

When Joanna had made her exit, Scott gave Tony's shoulder a squeeze. "Sorry about getting us into trouble."

"That's okay. She did more yelling at you than me." Tony glanced up at Scott, his mouth stretching into a mischievous grin. "Now that Mom's gone, could I try jousting with the lettuce?"

Scott laughed. "No way. Didn't you hear me promise your mother?"

Tony pleaded with his eyes.

"If she came in and caught us again, we'd really be in trouble."

Tony's silence was eloquent.

"All right," Scott finally agreed, albeit reluctantly. "Since this is your sixth birthday. But only one hit."

Joanna had just finished setting the table in the small dining area when the doorbell chimed. She greeted the Jacksons—Kathy, Beverly and her husband, Joe.

"Where's the birthday boy?" Kathy asked, surveying the living room.

"In the kitchen. He's supposed to be helping Scott make a salad."

"Hmm," Beverly intoned, handing Joanna a gaily wrapped package. "You two're becoming quite an item."

"We're good friends." Joanna failed to meet the six dark eyes staring at her as she took their lightweight wraps and hung them in the closet. "Have a seat," she invited. "Dinner should be ready shortly."

This time when she entered the kitchen, Tony was busy putting salad greens, diced green pepper, cucumbers and radishes in a bowl.

As Scott made a production out of tossing in the dressing, he murmured something she didn't catch, and Tony collapsed in a spasm of childish giggles. The scene sent a searing pain spiraling through Joanna. She stood rooted to the spot, unwilling to believe her own response.

Scott looked up and found her studying them. The smile died on his lips. "Are you all right?"

Guiltily, she jerked her head up. "I'm fine. Just thinking."

Scott hitched his chin toward Tony. "We make a super team, don't we?"

"Yes." She moved toward the stove. "A super team."

When they'd finished their task, Scott gave Tony a playful clip on the jaw. "I'll bet this'll be the best salad anyone's ever tasted."

Joanna opened a drawer and got out the oven mitts. "If Tony had his way, we wouldn't be having salad tonight. Or, for that matter, the green beans and fresh fruit. We'd be making do with the fried chicken, macaroni-and-cheese and cake with ice cream."

Scott grinned. "Sounds like a winning combination to me. Food that's tasty and food that's healthy."

"You never run out of tact, do you?"

"What can I say? Principals never leave school without it."

Unaccountably irritated, she snapped, "How convenient," then glanced at Tony. "Honey, would you help me—"

"I want to stay here with Coach Hartman."

Again, Joanna felt her insides shrivel. This time she couldn't deny the emotion. Jealousy. But what, she admonished herself, did she have to be jealous of? The special relationship that was developing between her son and his principal?

Or was the green-eyed monster directed more at Scott? Did she fear he was supplanting her in Tony's affections? That she was becoming a third wheel?

Whatever, the reaction made her feel small, petty. With an effort, she beat it down and pasted a bright smile on her face. "Very well, give Coach Hartman a hand if you like. But be sure you do what he says. No goofing off."

Scott, who'd picked up on the disturbing vibes, told Tony, "For starters, you might take the salad to the table."

"If I drop it, I won't have to eat it."

"You do," Joanna warned, "and I'll send you straight to your room. Even if this is your birthday."

"I was only kidding, Mom." Carefully, he picked up the bowl and carried it into the dining area.

"Is anything wrong, Jo?" Scott asked.

She whirled around as if she'd been struck. "What could possibly be wrong?"

"I don't know. But you seem to be a trifle edgy. Nervous about the dinner party?"

"Don't be ridiculous." She seized the platter of chicken in one hand and the basket of rolls in the other. "Let's eat."

The dinner was an unqualified success. But no one would have known it to watch Joanna. She took a helping from each dish but ended up mostly scooting the food around on her plate.

Fortunately, she didn't have to offer much in the way of small talk. As usual, Beverly kept up a constant stream of chatter, filling everyone in on the latest happenings in the apartment complex. Ordinarily Joanna found her neighbor's nose for news amusing, but tonight she had to force her laughter rather than let it come naturally.

Scott and Joe Jackson discovered that they shared an interest in the Philadelphia Phillies and spent a lot of time rehashing the past season. Both agreed that if the team hadn't suffered so many injuries, they would have again made it to the World Series. Tony, with his keen interest in sports, contributed a few comments to the adult conversation.

Which left Kathy. She didn't have much interest in the table talk, but that apparently didn't bother her a whit. She seemed content to bask in the glory of having dinner with the indubitably gorgeous Scott Hartman. She could scarcely drag her eyes away from him. Which was no mean feat, considering she was eating at the same time. More than once, her fork nearly missed her mouth. Privately entertained, Joanna could hear the teenager breathlessly recounting every detail of the evening to her friends.

Joanna's only regret was that there were no children Tony's age present. She'd planned to ask some of the soccer-team members but felt she couldn't invite one without including them all, and the apartment was too small for a kiddie party. So she'd settled for adults, hoping that by next year Tony would have made some close friends.

When it seemed that everyone had finished, Joanna slid back her chair. "I'll clear the dishes and get the coffee started."

"Let me help," Scott offered.

While Joanna stacked plates, Scott transported leftovers to the kitchen.

"You two make a good-looking couple," Beverly announced casually the second Scott was out of earshot.

Joanna gasped at her neighbor's frankness and dropped the salt shaker she'd just picked up, spilling the contents on the now not-so-clean linen cloth. Automatically, she took a pinch of the white crystals and tossed them over a shoulder.

Beverly assessed her with disbelieving eyes. "Don't tell me you're superstitious."

"Whatever gave you that idea?" Joanna hedged.

"That little maneuver with the salt."

"Oh, that." Joanna shrugged. "Insurance."

"Come again?"

"A mere precaution. Since chance has a nasty way of playing tricks."

"Mumbo jumbo," Beverly pronounced with a dismissive wave.

Scott returned to the dining area on time to hear the comment. Joanna allotted him a brief glance, then zeroed in on her neighbor. "You know I don't actually believe all that stuff about walking under ladders or black cats crossing your path—"

"Or throwing spilled salt over your shoulder," Beverly inserted dryly.

"That either. But at the same time, I figure what's the harm? It's not nice to challenge Lady Luck," Joanna tacked on, distorting the words of a popular commercial.

Scott chuckled. "Come on, Joanna. You sound like the woman who says she's a little pregnant. Either she is or she isn't. 'Fess up. You believe in hocus-pocus or you don't."

"Well, I suppose, if I were forced to make a choice, I suppose I...do." She dropped her gaze as if she'd just admitted to committing a capital crime.

"*I...do,*" Beverly echoed. "Now that's one of the nicest little phrases in the English language."

Bright color blotched Joanna's face. The warning glance she threw Beverly told her that that subject was definitely off limits. "Anyway, if you think I'm a little strange, you're bound to think my whole family's crazy."

Beverly squinted skeptically. "Your entire family?"

"So I exaggerate. All the same, Aunt Julia won't step out of the house before consulting her tarot cards, while Uncle Bert reads his tea leaves every morning after breakfast. Compared to that, what's a little salt over the shoulder?" She started toward the kitchen, effectively cutting off further discussion of what she considered a touchy subject. Silly little rituals were one thing, but what bothered Joanna was darker, more ominous. She couldn't shake the belief that luck was against her, that fate was waiting around the corner, ready to trip her up. "I'm going to plug in the coffee," she announced to no one in particular.

Less than two minutes later she came back through the door, carrying a birthday cake decorated with miniature soccer players, one kicking a black-and-white ball into a tiny net. The tableau was surrounded by six lighted candles.

At that point everyone broke into "Happy Birthday," which ended in a round of applause when Tony extinguished his candles with a single blow.

"What did you wish for?" Kathy asked.

"I can't tell or it won't come true."

Scott leaned over and mumbled into Joanna's ear. "I wonder where that particular bit of lore came from?"

"I have no idea," she equivocated, fixing her gaze on Tony. How could she make Scott understand that she wasn't superstitious so much as she was reluctant to take chances?

Beverly picked up the silver cutter resting on the edge of the cake stand. "Why don't I take care of this, Joanna, while you serve the coffee?"

After Tony had enjoyed seconds of the chocolate layer cake, his mother gathered several gifts from the hall closet and laid them on the table beside those their guests had brought.

"All of these for me?" Tony asked with obvious pleasure.

"For you."

He dove into the first package, pieces of wrapping flying every which way. "Oh, boy! Look, Mom. A soccer ball!"

"How nice! Who's it from?"

He ripped open the card and handed it to Joanna, who read aloud, "The Jacksons. What do you say, Tony?"

"Thank you, Mr. and Mrs. Jackson. You, too, Kathy."

"You're welcome," Beverly responded on behalf of her family. "Since your coach here says you're quite a player, we thought you'd like to get in some extra practice."

The next present, a popular board game, was from Joanna's sister Lois in Los Angeles. The Mansfields, who had called earlier in the day with their birthday greetings, had mailed the third gift. Tony was delighted to discover that it contained a toy filling station crafted by his grandfather and several small cars from his grandmother.

To cover the fact nothing had arrived from Mike's parents, Joanna gave Tony only enough time to service one of the miniature autos before she handed him her package. She'd decided on a new pair of jeans and an Eagles sweatshirt.

In contrast to the first four boxes that could have been vying for the title of best-dressed gift, the last bore a remarkable resemblance to ten pounds of hamburger wrapped by a butcher. "Not the neatest job in the world," Scott apologized, "but I hope you like what's inside."

When Tony pulled out a soft, gray-striped toy kitten, he let out a squeal of pleasure and clutched the small animal to his chest. "Just like Miss Kitty."

"When you pull the bell on her collar," Scott said, "her head and tail move. I thought she might be a good substitute until your mother decides you can have the real thing."

The rest of the evening was passed in pleasant conversation. At ten-thirty, Joanna walked over to her son, who was playing with his new toys. "I hate to be a party pooper and put an end to all your fun, but I think you'd better get your bath and hop into your pjs."

"Ah, Mom, do I hav'ta? Can't I stay up a little longer? It's my birthday."

"I'm afraid not. It's already well past your bedtime."

Scott reached down and tweaked Tony's ear. "Tell you what. You do as your mother says. Maybe if we're both real good, she'll let me read you a story."

"Oh, boy! Can he, Mom, can he?"

"May he," Joanna corrected. "You're seeking permission, so you should say 'may he.'"

"Whatever." Tony looked at Joanna with imploring eyes. "Can he?" he asked, his grammar lesson obviously not sinking in.

Joanna gave up—on both counts—and smiled at her son. "If the story isn't too long."

Without another word, Tony scampered off in the direction of the bathroom. Before he could zoom by Joanna, she grabbed him by the seat of his pants. "Whoa, mister," she whispered. "Before you complete your disappearing act, what do you say to the Jacksons?"

Tony's expression was bewildered. "Good night?"

"Try again." She spoke next to his ear. "It has something to do with good manners."

"Oh, I know." He turned toward their next-door neighbors, a cherubic smile curving his mouth. "Thank you, Mr. and Mrs. Jackson and Kathy, for coming to my party. And for the soccer ball. I'm sure it'll bring me many hours of enjoyment."

His dues to politeness paid, Tony spun on a heel and dashed down the hall. When the four adults and one teenager heard the door click, they nearly convulsed with smothered laughter.

"Where on earth did he learn a speech like that?" Beverly sputtered.

Joanna shook her head in amazement. "I have no idea. I've tried to teach him to say his pleases and thank-yous, but I swear I've never coached him to sound like Little Lord Fauntleroy."

As if they were of one mind, Beverly and Joe rose. "I think the three of us should take our cue from Tony," Beverly said. "It's time we said our thank-yous, too. Kathy and I have to be up bright and early to heat up the plastic." At Joanna's quizzical frown, she explained, "The charge cards. As you undoubtedly know, Wilkins' is having a sale."

Joe emitted a long-suffering groan. "I thought you took Kathy shopping last week."

"But that was for shoes, skirts and sweaters."

"Plus a jacket," his daughter guilelessly added. "I still need a winter coat, Dad."

Joe looked at Scott. "You're lucky not to have a teenage daughter. They seem to think their old man's wallet is a bank vault."

"My sympathy," Scott returned.

Only Joanna detected the remoteness in his voice and the taut lines around his mouth. "Thanks again for helping Tony celebrate," she told the Jacksons. "He specifically asked that the three of you and Scott be included on the guest list."

"We feel honored," Beverly said, stepping out the door Joe had opened for her. "See you tomorrow."

Once they were gone, Joanna turned to Scott. "Could I fix you a drink before I check on the birthday boy and start the dishes?"

"I don't need a thing."

"Then excuse me a minute."

As she veered toward the bathroom, Scott blocked her way. "I have a better idea. Why don't you sit down and prop up your feet while I make sure Tony isn't turning the tub into an Olympic pool. I'll help you with the cleanup later."

"But," Joanna protested, "you're company."

"And you're tired. Birthday parties might be fun, but they're also work."

Though Joanna enjoyed being pampered, she didn't rest long before she tackled the dishes. It was pleasant having a man around to look after Tony while she restored order in the kitchen—a welcome reprieve from the necessity of handling everything herself. She had finished loading the last of the dirty cups and plates into the dishwasher when Scott came through the door.

"Tony's having a grand time with the bubble bath, pretending to be Santa Claus. He piles on the lather, then shaves off his beard." Scott nodded toward the sink. "Can... *may* I help?"

Joanna grinned. "No. The only thing left to scrub is the electric fry pan, but I'll let it soak for an hour or so first." She wiped her hands on a towel. "Are you sure you want to stick around to read Tony a story? If you don't, I'm sure he'll understand."

"A promise is a promise."

Leaving Tony to finish his lengthy bath and get ready for bed, Joanna and Scott returned to the living room. Alone with him for the first time since their camping trip, she felt awkward. While he took a seat on the couch, she surveyed the room. Besides keeping an eye on Tony, he'd folded the wrapping paper in a neat pile, plumped up the pillows and cushions and put everything back in order. Joanna was touched. "Thanks for the maid service. I really appreciate it. And that's a nice touch—displaying Tony's cards on the mantle."

"I wanted to be sure none got thrown out by mistake."

Scott rested an arm along the top of the sofa and crossed an ankle over his knee. Though the position was casual, masculine vitality seemed to radiate from him. Suddenly, Joanna's body felt as electrically charged as the atmosphere just before a storm. Taking the easy chair opposite him, she tried, without complete success, to blot out the memory of his firm hands exploring her body. In an attempt to relax, she asked casually, "Are you positive I can't interest you in a drink? Or another cup of coffee?"

"No thanks." He sent her an easy smile. "I have to give you credit, Joanna."

"For what?"

"As I was straightening up the living room, I realized that I've never told you how much I like what you've done here. You've taken an ordinary apartment and made it into a real home."

She laughed. "You must be joking."

"I couldn't be more serious."

"Practically everything you see I picked up for a song. You don't exactly end up with something that could appear on the pages of *House Beautiful* when you buy at red-tag sales."

"I'm not talking about the furniture—but all the little touches that make the place so warm and cozy. Like this." He leaned over and picked up a colorful ceramic bowl from the coffee table.

Joanna's smile was sad. "Mike bought that for me on our honeymoon."

For a few seconds Scott said nothing. Finally, when the silence had become so intense that it could be cut with a knife, he remarked, "Tell me about him."

"Mike? What—what would you like to know?"

"How you met, what kind of person he was. The usual."

Joanna hugged her arms to her chest. For two years she'd tried not to think much about Mike. The memory of him filled her with too much pain. But she also knew Scott wouldn't be satisfied until he had some

GET YOUR GIFTS FROM SILHOUETTE®
ABSOLUTELY FREE!

Mail this card today!

Printed in the U.S.A.
© 1990 HARLEQUIN ENTERPRISES LIMITED

PLACE
JOKER
STICKER
HERE

PLAY THIS CARD RIGHT!

YES! Please send me my 4 Silhouette Special Edition® novels FREE along with my free Gold-Plated Chain and free mystery gift. I wish to receive all the benefits of the Silhouette Reader Service™ as explained on the opposite page.

(C-SIL-SE-11/90) 335 CIS 8168

NAME _____
(PLEASE PRINT)

ADDRESS _____ APT. _____

CITY _____

PROV. _____ POSTAL CODE _____

Offer limited to one per household and not valid to current Silhouette Special Edition subscribers. All orders subject to approval.

SILHOUETTE READER SERVICE "NO RISK" GUARANTEE

- There's no obligation to buy—and the free books remain yours to keep.
- You pay the low subscribers-only price and receive books before they appear in stores.
- You may end your subscription anytime—just write and let us know or return any shipment to us at our cost.

IT'S NO JOKE!

MAIL THE POSTPAID CARD AND
GET FREE GIFTS AND $11.80 WORTH OF
SILHOUETTE NOVELS—FREE!

If offer card is missing, write to:
Silhouette Reader Service, P.O. Box 609, Fort Erie, Ontario L2A 5X3

**Business
Reply Mail**

No Postage Stamp
Necessary if Mailed
in Canada

Postage will be paid by

**SILHOUETTE
READER SERVICE
P.O. BOX 609
FORT ERIE, ONTARIO
L2A 9Z9**

Canada Post
125
Postes Canada

answers to his questions. She prayed that she had the strength to give him enough to assuage his curiosity before diverting the conversation to some other topic.

Joanna rolled her bottom lip between her teeth. "I met Mike my freshman year at Empire State College. We ran into each other. Literally. As luck would have it, my very first class was an eight o'clock, but I didn't hear the alarm go off. It was quarter to eight when my eyes finally popped open." She chuckled. "I pulled on my clothes in ten seconds flat, finger-combed my hair and grabbed up my books. I was still going a hundred miles an hour when I zoomed around the corner of Jamison Hall and collided with Mike."

"Of course he wrapped his arms around you to keep you from falling."

"On the contrary, he was as startled as I was. Much to my chagrin, I landed on my backside. Mike helped me up, but I had the wind knocked out of me and could barely speak. He wanted to take me to the health center—he was a pretty big obstacle to crash into—but I assured him I was fine, so we went to the student union for a cup of coffee instead. I was reluctant to skip class—scared's more like it—but he insisted missing it completely would be better than walking in fifteen minutes late. According to Mike, professors were notorious egotists who believed the universe revolved around their lectures. I shouldn't interrupt one since the profs considered them sacrosanct. I wasn't sure what *sacrosanct* meant, so I went along with him."

"And so he managed to sweep you off your feet?"

"In a manner of speaking, yes. I'd never dated much. The guys at my high school were generally nerds, jocks or delinquents. I avoided all three."

"But I thought Mike played football."

"He did. It just wasn't his whole life. The ancient Greeks emphasized a good mind in a sound body. That was Mike. He was both a superb athlete and an outstanding scholar. But he didn't confine his interests to any one area. He'd decided to major in computer science because he felt computers were the wave of the future. Yet he didn't ignore the humanities. Which I'm primarily interested in. He was as happy as I to spend our honeymoon in New England sightseeing and going to museums." She reached out and ran her fingers over the ceramic piece. "Mike found this in one of the museum shops. He said it reminded him of me. Solid and practical but at the same time fiery and—" Joanna broke off, her face coloring.

Getting to her feet, she excused herself. "I'd better make sure Tony brushes his teeth."

Without a comment Scott let her go. For weeks he'd wondered about the man Joanna had shared her life with. Ironically, now that he had a thumbnail sketch, he wished he'd kept his curiosity at bay. Scott considered himself a pretty average guy. How could he compete with a veritable legend? He was so mired in depression that he wasn't aware that Tony had come into the room until he felt a tug on his sleeve.

"I'm ready for my story."

Scott followed Tony down the hall to his room. Walking through the door, he reflected on what a good job Joanna had done here, too. It was a boy's paradise. An NFL-print spread covered the bed and matching curtains hung at the windows. Taped to the walls were posters of sports figures. In one corner sat a small combination radio, record and cassette player and in another a model of a space station. Tony's birthday gifts lay haphazardly on a small play table. Wooden shelves were lined with books. At a glance Scott could tell most were dog-eared because they'd been thumbed through so many times. On the nightstand stood a small framed snapshot of an elderly couple—most likely his grandparents—and a formal portrait of a handsome younger man. Mike?

Determined not to look further, Scott directed his eyes to the books. "Which one should we read?" Tony pulled a slender volume from the shelf in front of him and handed it to Scott.

"Do you want to hop into bed or should we sit in the rocking chair?"

"It's not big enough. We wouldn't fit."

"We would if you sat on my lap." Tony looked up and, wordlessly taking Scott by the hand, led him to the antique rocker.

That's where Joanna found them twenty minutes later. Miss Kitty's look-alike was clutched in Tony's arms. Standing in the doorway, Joanna listened to Scott's deep baritone recounting the tale of a little boy who suffered unspeakable terrors because his room was filled with monsters. He was in agony until a kindly older man proved to him they were purely the products of his imagination. For the past two years the story had been one of Tony's favorites.

As she waited quietly by the door, Tony's head fell back against Scott's chest. His eyes closed, then opened, then closed again. For a time Scott read on. When he was certain the boy was asleep, he shut the book and set it aside. Holding Tony in the crook of one arm, he pulled back the bedding with the other and carefully slid him between the sheets. After tucking the covers under the little fellow's chin, he bent and lightly touched his lips to the narrow forehead. In his sleep Tony hugged the stuffed animal tighter and gave a contented sigh.

Jealousy once again reared its ugly head. But this time, to Joanna's dismay, the object was her own son. She longed to be the one curled up in Scott's lap, the one his gentle hands slid into bed, the one his lips tenderly kissed.

Her envy soon gave way to pangs of guilt and finally to a wave of loneliness. She wondered what Scott would say, what he would do if she should ask him to share her bed.

Maybe all this talk about Mike had stirred her physical needs, making her long for a warm body to reach for in the middle of the night. But Joanna knew better. If she were honest with herself, it wasn't memories of Mike but Scott himself who'd awakened her sexuality. She knew in a flash that it would be best if he left. She could never give her body without giving her heart into the bargain.

But she couldn't fall in love again.

As the tall man lingered at Tony's bedside, Joanna straightened her spine and went into the room to offer a silent good-night to her son.

Chapter Eight

The following Tuesday, Joanna was propped up in bed, studying a computer manual for a new spreadsheet program. She was reading for the umpteenth time the section on configuring print graphs to system hardware, and still hadn't sorted out the commands, when her doorbell sounded.

Joanna's heart leaped to her throat. The clock on the dresser read twelve-thirty, and for her, calls after midnight signaled disaster.

She grabbed her robe but couldn't seem to make her fingers move fast enough. What if something terrible had happened to her parents? The thought was too awful to contemplate.

Joanna rushed through the apartment. All she could envision was a highway patrolman waiting to inform her of a terrible accident. Her fingers were trembling so badly that she finally gave up on belting the sash of her kimono. With a perfunctory glance through the peephole, she pushed back the bolt and flung open the door.

When her eyes lit on her former boss, Joanna's adrenaline high instantly plummeted and she sagged against the door frame. "Dwayne Simmons. What are you doing here?"

Dwayne's cocky smile didn't waver a fraction of an inch. "Is that any way to greet an old friend? Anybody'd think you weren't glad to see me."

"Who's awake to notice?" she countered, tactfully refusing to acknowledge the truth of his statement. "Do you have any idea what time it is?"

He consulted his expensive gold watch. "Exactly 12:32."

"Doesn't that tell you something?"

"Is it supposed to?"

Joanna's frustrated grunt came through gritted teeth. "Most people are asleep at this hour. You got me out of bed, Dwayne."

"I'm only too aware of that." His gaze dropped to her chest. "Aren't you going to invite me in?"

She followed the direction of his eyes. Appalled at how much the wide gap in her robe revealed, she yanked the lapels together. "No," she bit out, fast losing patience. "I hadn't considered it."

Still smiling, he flattened a palm against her door-jamb in the style of a debonair movie idol. "Let's not be hasty."

Joanna ran a hand through her hair. "Must I be blunt? You're not welcome here. Particularly not in the middle of the night."

"Even if I can't find a room in all of Philadelphia?"

"You'll pardon me if I don't fall for that line."

"It's true," he said, his expression a study in practiced innocence.

"You expect me to believe that out of the hundreds of hotels and motels in this entire city you can't find a single vacancy?"

"You got it," he singsonged.

"Impossible!"

"Haven't you read the papers? This week alone there are VFW, DAR and AMA conventions, not to mention conferences for writers and health-care workers. My plight is desperate."

Joanna responded with an unladylike snort. "How did you find me? I'm not in the phone book."

"A friend in personnel was most cooperative."

"Female, no doubt." Joanna crossed her arms over her chest. "You came here without a reservation, didn't you? Whatever made you think I'd put you up?"

Dwayne let his high-voltage smile—one expressly designed to send female hearts into a tailspin—speak for him.

"Don't waste your charm on me, Dwayne. I'm immune."

"Not immune. Stubborn. I expected by now you'd have some regrets about not giving the two of us a chance."

"Sorry to disappoint you." She started to close the door, but Dwayne was too quick for her. He put out a hand and wedged a knee between it and the frame. "Still playing hard to get, huh?"

Joanna's heart beat faster. She was keenly aware of her state of undress. In a mollifying voice, she begged, "Please don't do this. Go away, Dwayne."

"Believe me, I would if I could, but I don't have a place to stay. And it's not my fault. Which I'll explain if you give me a chance. How about it? One night? A favor," he wheedled. "Remember, you owe me."

"That's low, Dwayne, resorting to . . . to blackmail because you approved that salary increase. Need I remind you that I *deserved* it?"

"You also *needed* it."

Joanna vacillated, lamenting that her sense of honor should include the likes of Dwayne Simmons. Never mind his motives. He had come to her financial rescue, and she felt in his debt. "I really shouldn't, but—"

"You will." He took advantage of her hesitation to sidle past her.

Because she hadn't budged an inch, Dwayne's chest nearly made contact with the tips of her breasts. She cringed and took two steps backward. "You managed that quite nicely, didn't you?"

Dwayne offered a satisfied grin. "I knew you were too decent to turn me away, Joanna. To square accounts, we'll have dinner tomorrow night."

"No, we won't."

"That remains to be seen," he muttered under his breath.

She planted both hands on her hips and angled her head questioningly. "What did you say?"

He waved a hand. "Nothing."

"I'll get you some sheets and blankets. You can sleep on the couch."

Joanna made short work of fixing up his bed. When she'd finished tucking in the last corner, she commented, "You never did say what brought you to Philadelphia. Without a room."

"Business. As for the hotel fiasco, that's Maguire's fault. He failed to have his secretary make a reservation."

"Mr. Maguire sent you?" she asked, mentioning Dwayne's immediate superior at Wilkins' New York headquarters.

"To conduct a time-management study in the Philadelphia store. I'll be here the next three weeks. And," he added, "guess who's going to be my temporary assistant?" When she didn't respond, he clarified, "You. I convinced the old goat it'd make my job a lot easier and quicker if I could have someone who was familiar with my work habits." He favored her with another of his engaging smiles. "If the truth were known, I could finish up here in half that time, but who am I to argue with the brass? If they say the job'll take three weeks, I'll stretch it to three weeks. I'm sure I can find something...to keep me occupied."

Joanna made no effort to hold onto her control. "Why did I ever let you through that door? I must have lost my mind." She stabbed a finger at his chest. "Listen to me, Dwayne Simmons. I may have no choice but to serve as your assistant, but if you think for one second I'm going to keep you entertained, you have another think coming. One reason I transferred from New York was to get away from you."

"You don't mean that."

"Will nothing discourage you?" Joanna moaned. She lifted her shoulders in defeat, realizing she might as well be talking to a brick wall. Dwayne's ego was so colossal, he couldn't imagine a woman who wasn't ready to fall on her knees for a few crumbs of his attention.

Better to deal with him in the morning when she was rested and had her wits about her. "I'll see you bright and early," she said, pivoting toward the hall.

"Not too early, I hope. Getting up before seven is positively uncivilized."

"Six o'clock sharp. That's when I'll be rolling you out. And," she continued pointedly, "if necessary, you can spend the day on the phone finding a room."

Thirty minutes later, Joanna lay in her bed, wide awake and feeling a little guilty. Why she should be the one to suffer pangs of conscience for her sharp tongue, she didn't know. But it wasn't in her nature to hurt others, even someone as egotistical as Dwayne Simmons. If only the snake would take a hint, she wouldn't be forced to make such cutting remarks!

Joanna had just turned over and closed her eyes when she thought she heard her doorknob rattle slightly. Before she'd gone to bed, she'd taken the precaution of locking the door. At the time she'd told herself she was being foolish. Invading her bedroom was going too far—even for Dwayne.

Now she was grateful she hadn't heeded the impulse to trust him. Whether she was imagining things or not, it was better not to tempt fate.

Joanna partially lifted one eyelid and groped for the alarm clock on the nightstand. She'd set it a half hour early, wanting to make sure she had Dwayne off the living room couch and out the door before she wakened Tony.

"Time to rise and shine." She poked the long frame draped a good six inches over the arm of the couch and smiled to herself. A perverse part of her hoped her uninvited guest had spent a miserable night.

When Dwayne didn't respond to her light prod, she leaned over and vigorously shook his shoulder. He jackknifed straight up. "What—what is it?" he blurted, oscillating his head as if he were disoriented.

Joanna's eyes ranged over the thick mat of dark hair on his chest, then lowered to the sheet and blanket draped low over his lean hips. It was apparent that he'd slept in the raw. Her gaze sought the neutral territory of the floor as a wolfish glint lit Dwayne's eyes. Damn the man's narcissistic hide! He'd assumed she'd been aroused by the perusal of his body rather than revolted by his crassness!

"I don't want Tony to find you here. You have ten minutes to shower, dress and split."

"No breakfast, no—"

"No nothing. You can grab a cup of coffee at the all-night café near Wilkins'." She straightened and stepped back. "I don't know what it takes to get through to you, Dwayne, but I'm not interested in a relationship."

"That's what attracts me to you, Joanna. You're so shy."

"Would a timid person be this frank? Read my lips, Dwayne—I'm not in the least attracted to you. In the future I'll thank you to take your dubious charms elsewhere."

"You really know how to turn a guy on, don't you?"

Exasperated, Joanna closed her eyes. "I'm not trying to turn you on. When will you get it through your thick head that I want to turn you *off*?"

"You can't fool me. You're hoping to pique my interest by playing coy."

"Can it, Dwayne. You're wasting my time and yours." Gesturing toward the clock, she warned him, "Now, you have only five minutes to get out of here."

"Okay. For now."

"Forever," Joanna amended wearily. She started to say something else but swallowed the words. She'd have more success reasoning with an amoeba than she would with Dwayne Simmons!

As he whipped back the covers, Joanna whirled and fled to her room where she remained for the next ten minutes. She thought she heard her front door open and close and prayed her ears hadn't deceived her. Finally, she got up enough nerve to peek into the hall. With Dwayne nowhere in sight she tiptoed down the corridor. He wasn't in the bathroom, nor the living room.

Sighing with relief, Joanna collapsed onto a chair. She'd give herself a few minutes to regain her composure before she went in to awaken Tony.

"Hi, Mom," Tony yelled from his spot a mere twelve inches from the TV.

"How many times have I told you not to sit so close to that screen!" Joanna returned as she hung up her coat in the hall closet.

"Did you have a rotten day, too?"

At her son's words, Joanna's heart began to thump. Something about his tone disturbed her. "What was so bad about your day, honey?"

"We had tomato soup for lunch."

"Is that all? Tomato soup?" She held onto her breath, waiting for his answer.

"You know how we're supposed to eat everything."

Joanna knelt beside him on the floor. "Yes."

"I wadded up my napkin and put it in the soup bowl. To hide what I left. I hate tomato soup," he disclosed unnecessarily.

"And?"

"I sneaked my tray past Mrs. Drummond, but when I went to slide it on the belt, it slipped." Tony gave his mother a sheepish look. "I spilled soup all over my new jeans."

Joanna was so relieved that she had to suppress a grin. "No big deal. They'll wash."

"That's not all. Mrs. Drummond was mad. Chris— he's my new friend... Oh, I almost forgot. He asked me over to play after supper. You can call his mom. Anyway, Chris said Mrs. Drummond was madder'n a hornet. What's a hornet, Mom?"

"A hornet's sort of like a bee," she explained, looking down at him and noting that he'd changed into his after-school clothes. "What did you do with your jeans?"

"Kathy put 'em in the sink to soak. Mrs. Drummond sent me and Chris to the boys' room and we used paper towels, but I couldn't get it all off." He wrinkled his nose. "My jeans smell like rotten tomatoes."

"I suppose it could have been worse." Joanna rose and took a step toward the hallway, then turned and asked, "Where's Kathy now?"

"On the phone in your bedroom. I think it's her boyfriend." Tony rolled his eyes in disgust.

"How long have they been talking?"

"Forever."

"I'll give her another five minutes before I chase her out. I'd like to change before I start dinner. How about spaghetti tonight?"

"Yippee!" Tony shouted.

Joanna headed toward the kitchen, genuinely smiling for the first time that day. Without a doubt, her son would find it no hardship if he had to exist exclusively on pasta.

* * *

"Not you again," Joanna clipped out. She'd just finished the dishes, and with Tony over at Chris's, she'd planned on catching the evening news on TV.

"I knew you'd be happy to see me," Dwayne commented, dismissing her sarcasm.

"After today, if I never saw you again, it would be too soon."

And that was the truth. Joanna had harbored a small hope of wriggling out of her new assignment, but it seemed that Maguire had contacted Steve Graham, her present supervisor, who had obligingly cut back on Joanna's duties so she could be at Dwayne's beck and call. She thought he'd been persistent in New York, but that was only a taste of what had gone on from nine to five in the Philadelphia office.

If she hadn't needed this job to put a roof over her son's head, food on the table and clothes on both their backs, she'd have quit in a minute. Unfortunately, she couldn't—not unless she was willing to join the ranks of America's homeless.

Three weeks. Please, God, she prayed silently, please let them pass quickly. But in her heart she knew those twenty-one days would seem an eternity. She felt as if she were embarking on a prison sentence. Which, in a way, she was.

Dwayne delivered a light cuff to her chin. "What a kidder you are, Joanna."

"You won't be laughing when I slap you with a sexual-harassment suit," she threatened, although the thought of putting herself through that emotional meat grinder was almost more than she could bear.

To Joanna's complete amazement, Dwayne had the audacity to look bewildered, as if he couldn't believe what he was hearing. "If I thought for a minute you were serious," he noted in his velvety voice, "I'd back off. But I'm wise to you, Joanna. That's your way of leading me on." His face split in a wide grin. "Aren't you going to offer me a drink before I take you to dinner?"

"I've already eaten."

"But we had a date."

"Only in your mind. I never agreed to go out with you." What, Joanna pondered, would it take to blast through the man's denseness? Dynamite?

She was at her wit's end when, out of the corner of her eye, she caught a glimpse of Scott coming up the walk.

Not stopping to analyze the mix of emotions that coursed through her, Joanna called his name and ran out the door. Without thinking, she threw her arms around his neck and, before he could react, planted a kiss on his mouth.

Scott hadn't the vaguest notion what had gotten into Joanna, but he wasn't going to let an opportunity like this slip by. Ever since their impromptu camping trip, she'd been as spooked as an untamed horse.

When Joanna would have ended the kiss, Scott banded one arm around her shoulders, the other around her waist. Exerting pressure against the small of her back, he molded her against him and plunged his tongue between her parted lips. The maneuver effectively stifled her small whimper of protest.

Joanna went limp in his arms. She forgot where she was, even forgot about her audience of one. With a sureness that had her craving more, Scott took her beyond any thought at all, and she gave herself up to the moment.

It was a long time before the embrace ended and reality crept back into her consciousness. When it did, Joanna could barely find enough air to speak. At last she announced breathily, "I have company."

Scott had been oblivious to everything except Joanna's warm mouth on his. Only now did he remember seeing a man silhouetted in her doorway. Scott eyed him suspiciously.

"Come meet Dwayne Simmons. I was his secretary in New York." Still unsteady on her feet, she looped an arm through Scott's, and together they walked toward her apartment.

Maybe, Joanna considered, with another man around, Dwayne would decide to get lost. To her dismay, he remained right where he was. Loath to create a scene in front of Scott, she fashioned a smile, introduced the two and invited them inside. After they'd taken seats in her living room—Dwayne on the overstuffed chair, Scott on the couch—she asked, "Would either of you like coffee?"

The answer was a simultaneous "No."

"Very well." Automatically she claimed the space next to Scott. She folded her hands in her lap and watched as the two men kept silent, each taking careful measure of the other.

At last Scott remarked, "Joanna tells me she worked for you in New York."

"Right, worked for me. Among other things," Dwayne added in a silky voice.

Joanna did a slow burn at the subtle innuendo. She'd forgotten how her erstwhile boss thrived on male competition. Well, she'd be damned if she'd let him bait Scott by implying the two of them had been intimate.

Inching a tad closer to the man beside her, she noted pleasantly, "Those 'other things' included a lot of conferences for Wilkins'. Because the board liked to keep abreast of the latest developments in marketing, every employee was required to attend two meetings a year." For emphasis, she laid a hand on Scott's arm, but hurried on for fear that Dwayne would try to counter her. "Maybe I wouldn't have minded so much if we'd enjoyed nicer accommodations. But they always booked three women to a room at some budget hotel. As for a food allowance, unless we wanted to dig into our own pockets, we ate at the nearest greasy spoon."

Joanna tilted her head, frowning thoughtfully. "Come to think of it, though, I don't remember the two of us ever attending the same conference. Did we, Dwayne?" she asked, knowing she was taking a calculated risk by tossing him that question.

"Not that I recall," he allowed with an aristocratic sniff. "Since I'm in management, our budget isn't so anemic."

Joanna smiled. Dwayne was playing right into her hands. As she expected, he was much too vain to admit that the Wilkins' chain treated him any way except royally. Which went to prove they hadn't traveled in the same circles.

She was about to put this little skirmish into her win column when Dwayne commented, "I wasn't thinking as much of meetings as other...affairs. Like those big celebrations every Christmas. All that food and champagne—we had a good time, didn't we, Joanna?" He gave her a wink, which suggested far more than his words.

Reminding herself that she could win battles and still lose the war, Joanna remarked frostily, "Speak for yourself, Dwayne. I always arrived at those *office* parties as late as I could and left as early as possible. I've never found it terribly entertaining watching adults drink themselves into a stupor." She swiveled her head toward Scott. "If we weren't expected to put in an appearance, I'd never have bothered showing up."

Just as Joanna rose from the couch, saying that she wanted some coffee, even if the two men didn't, Tony barged through the front door.

"Hi, Coach."

"Hi yourself, Pele," Scott responded. "How's it going?"

"Okay. I was over at Chris's. I can walk to his house by myself, but his dad drove me home 'cause it's late."

Smiling at her son's newfound loquaciousness, Joanna remarked, "You remember Mr. Simmons, don't you, dear? From New York?"

The boy shook his head slowly back and forth, his face sober. Joanna could have kissed him! It occurred to her that here was the smoking gun, the ultimate proof that there never had been anything personal between her and Dwayne. Otherwise her son would be well acquainted with him.

She walked over and put her arm around Tony's shoulder. "No? Well, that's not surprising since you seldom saw Mr. Simmons." That was an understatement if there ever was one, Joanna reflected. She could recall only two occasions when their paths had crossed: both Fourth of July picnics that Wilkins' held annually for their employees and families.

"I'm hungry," Tony said.

Joanna glanced at the clock. "I guess it's not too early for your snack."

She retreated with Tony to the kitchen, where she put on water for a cup of instant decaf before pulling a carton of milk from the refrigerator and a sack of chocolate-chip cookies off the cabinet shelf. All the while she and Tony chatted about what he'd done at Chris's, the two men in the next room were at the back of her mind. She didn't want to leave them alone for long, though she was certain she'd managed to clip Dwayne's wings. Surely by now Scott realized he'd been fabricating their involvement.

Responding to the whistling teakettle, Joanna poured boiling water over the dark brown crystals she'd measured into a china cup. Though she would have liked to talk longer to Tony, she left him to finish his snack and took herself back into the living room.

Strong silence greeted her. Scott and Dwayne were glaring at each other, the tension nearly palpable. She didn't have a chance to sit down before Dwayne was on his feet, claiming an early appointment.

Joanna tried to hide her pleasure at his announcement. She set her cup on the coffee table and prepared to see him out, but he signaled her to be seated. When the door closed behind him, Joanna sat on the chair Dwayne had vacated, picked up her hot drink and met Scott's piercing gaze.

"What's going on?" he asked.

"Dwayne's meeting tomorrow? I haven't a clue."

"Don't play dumb, Jo. I'm talking about Simmons himself, not his damn business schedule."

She took a sip of coffee and nearly scalded her tongue. "Dwayne was . . . is a—"

"A what?"

"The most charitable word that comes to mind is *Lothario*."

"A regular ladies' man, huh?" Scott leaned forward, his elbows braced on his thighs, his hands between his knees. "How long has he been coming on to you?"

"It doesn't matter."

"How long?" he persisted.

She placed her cup on an end table. "If you must know—shortly after I went to work for Wilkins'. The moment he learned I was single. To Dwayne's credit, he does stick to unattached women." She gave a sardonic laugh. "*Stick*'s the operative word here."

"So I gathered. Ever since New York, you say. That's quite a while for a man to chase after a woman." He studied his clasped hands. "Without encouragement."

Joanna stared owlishly at Scott. After what he'd heard, how could he possibly believe she'd led Dwayne on? "Surely you don't think I'd... Not with a man like Dwayne Simmons!"

"It isn't an unreasonable assumption. He's good-looking, probably has plenty of money. I didn't miss the snazzy sports number with the New York plates parked out front—"

"Dwayne's had his share of success," she interrupted. "To tell the truth, he's got a sixth sense when it comes to business. Too bad," she tacked on with disdain, "he also has an ego that rivals the square footage of Alaska."

"Are you telling me you never dated this guy?"

"Dated him!" She cocked her head, her eyes flashing her contempt. "You know how I spell *jerk*? D-W-A-Y-N-E S-I-M-M-O-N-S. Which makes it more than a mere four-letter word."

"Then why did he spend the night with you?"

Joanna's cup clattered in her saucer. "Is that what he said?"

"Yes. He sort of let it slip—as if he'd made an unintentional blunder. Naturally, I called him a liar." Scott hesitated. "He was lying, wasn't he, Jo?"

Her gaze lowered to her lap. "No. But it's not what you think."

"What do I think?" he asked, his voice tight.

"That I should have sent him away." She combed her fingers through her hair. "But I couldn't. First off, he caught me when I was . . . vulnerable. It was around twelve-thirty, and it scares the living daylights out of me when the phone or doorbell rings that time of night. I always imagine the worst. It was such a relief to find out nothing was wrong that I . . . well . . . I guess I let down my guard. Then, too, Dwayne once recommended me for a raise when I really needed the money, so I felt . . . obligated."

"How obligated?"

Color scalded her cheeks, but her tone was frigid. "He slept on the couch."

The door leading into the kitchen slowly opened, and Tony poked his head through. "Is it all right to come out now?"

Joanna regarded him with a puzzled frown. "Whatever made you think you couldn't?"

"You sounded madder than a hornet. Are you having a fight?"

Despite her agitation, she smiled. "Certainly not, Tony. We weren't arguing. We were merely . . ."

"Having a lively discussion, sport," Scott finished for her.

"Sounded like a fight to me."

"Are you ready to settle in for the night?" Joanna asked, ignoring Scott's disclaimer.

Tony padded into the living room and stood beside his mother's chair. "Will you read me a story?"

She glanced at Scott, whose imperceptible nod indicated for her to go ahead. "If we make it a short one.

And if you skip your bath until morning. It's already half an hour past your usual bedtime."

Fifteen minutes later Joanna returned and sank onto the chair across from Scott. "You never told me why you stopped in tonight," she remarked, hoping to close the subject of Dwayne Simmons. "Was there something about Tony you wanted to discuss?"

His eyes bored into hers. "Is that what you think? That I come here only because I'm interested in your son?"

Her mouth went dry. "Well...I assumed..."

"If you need me to spell it out again, Jo, I will. I'm here so often not solely because of my interest in Tony. I'm also interested in you. I'd like us to have a relationship, too. And by *relationship*, I don't mean as in parent-teacher."

Joanna sat very still. "I don't think that's a good idea."

His laugh was harsh. "God, Jo, I can't figure you! Not an hour ago you were kissing me like there wasn't going to be a tomorrow, letting me pull you so close a mosquito couldn't have found its way between us, clutching my arm like...I thought that at last we were getting somewhere."

She blanched. "I—I didn't mean to give you the wrong impression. It was...just...I was so happy to see you."

"Why?"

"I don't know. Because Dwayne was here and—"

"Oh, I get the picture. That little display of affection was for Simmons's benefit. Your way of telling him to beat it—you had someone else."

"No!" she protested. "I wouldn't use you like that!"

For a long moment, Joanna stared at him as she examined her motives. Could she actually have—at least on an unconscious level—cozied up to Scott to make a statement? She supposed it was within the realm of possibility. A stab of guilt kept her silent.

"If I'm not mistaken, Simmons got the message." Scott's voice faded as his eyes closed and reopened. "What a sap I've been!" He rose slowly, his shoulders slumped as if he'd been dealt a devastating blow. "I know when I've been had, Joanna. And I don't like the feeling. If you can't handle Simmons, you'll have to find yourself some other patsy. Don't expect me to play watchdog for you." He started toward the door, then paused. His back still to her, he asked, "Was he so wonderful that no other man will ever measure up?"

"Dwayne?" she babbled, too numb to think straight.

"No, Mike," he supplied, wheeling to face her.

The name of her dead husband was like a dash of cold water, instantly banishing the cobwebs from her brain. Joanna got to her feet. How was she supposed to answer a question like that? Like all couples, they'd had their individual shortcomings, but to air Mike's faults with another man struck her as a kind of betrayal. At length, she murmured, "What Mike and I shared is private."

"Strictly off limits, huh?" At the curt nod of her head, he asked, "In two long years, haven't you once been tempted by another man?"

"No," she lied, knowing full well how she was drawn to the one before her.

"Then you're still clinging to the past, Jo."

"That's not true!"

"Prove it. Let go of your husband and get on with your life. Allow someone else to share it. I know you better than you think. You're not a woman who prefers living alone, who enjoys celibacy. You can't tell me you are! There's too much passion in you, Jo. Too much you have to give." Swiftly he closed the distance between them and grasped her by the shoulders. "I was with you on the bank of that stream. You were as aroused as I was. Nothing you can say will make me believe otherwise."

"I wouldn't expect you to understand. It's late, Scott. You'd better leave."

His hands fell to his sides. "If that's what you want. But take my advice, Jo. I can understand why you don't want to get tangled up with Simmons. I'll accept—albeit grudgingly—that I'm not your type, either. But don't close yourself off from every man you meet. Find someone you can be happy with."

"Oh, you're great at running other people's lives, aren't you, *Dr.* Hartman? Why haven't you taken your own advice and found another wife?"

"It wasn't for lack of trying. But when the right woman came along—" He broke off. "I'm afraid the feeling's one-sided."

His last words were like a punch in the stomach, robbing Joanna of breath. "Scott, I've never offered you any encouragement."

"No, but like a fool, I hoped." Again he turned toward the door.

His eyes were so filled with hurt that Joanna couldn't let him leave without confessing the truth. "Scott, wait! Don't go!" She put a hand on his arm. "If I allowed myself, I could love you. I could fall hard. But I can't let that happen. Not because I think you don't measure up to Mike. You could...do. Maybe...maybe you're even more than..."

He twisted to face her. "Then what's the problem?"

"I'm afraid."

"Afraid? Of what?"

"To be happy."

For an instant, he merely stared. "That's crazy."

She shook her head as tears scalded her eyelids. "I know how it sounds. But don't you see? I can't take the chance of being hurt again."

"Just living is a risk, Jo. People get hurt every day. In little ways and big ones. That's life. It's no good trying to insulate yourself against pain. You might as well stop breathing."

"Maybe so, but you can hedge your losses."

"Funny, I never took you for a coward."

"An obvious misjudgment," she choked out.

"Is playing it safe that important to you?"

"Yes." Her chin wobbled. "I'm sorry."

"So am I."

She directed her gaze to a spot on the wall above his shoulder. "Goodbye, Scott."

"Not so fast." He dragged her to him. "Here's something to remember me by."

His lips came down on hers in a hard, crushing kiss. With all the strength she could muster, Joanna pushed at his shoulders, his chest, but Scott's arms were like iron chains binding her body to his. Within seconds, her heart was thundering, her blood pounding. Desire—hot and urgent—pulsed through her.

Of their own accord, her fingers twined about his neck, and she arched her body, fitting it more tightly to his. Only then did the quality of the kiss change. No longer harsh and demanding, Scott's lips softly seduced her to open to him. On a helpless little cry, she surrendered, and his tongue plumbed the depths of her mouth.

Joanna's senses were spinning. Everything about the kiss demanded her complete attention. She savored each distinct flavor, each subtle nuance of movement. Gently persuasive, Scott's embrace had her insides quivering. When his legs parted, straddling her thighs and molding her against his hardened flesh, she felt faint with need.

Suddenly a groan escaped him and he tore his mouth from hers. Before she could regain even a semblance of equilibrium, he'd snatched open the door and was gone.

For a moment—moments—Joanna stared vacantly into space. Gradually the wooden panels on her closed door came into focus. She blinked at the starkness of their square-cut patterns, and once more her vision clouded.

Soundlessly the tears she'd been holding back spilled over and stole down her cheeks.

Chapter Nine

Sitting behind her desk, Joanna dabbed at her runny nose and red-rimmed eyes. The day after her angry confrontation with Scott, she'd come down with a miserable cold, which, in a crazy sort of way, she considered fortunate. It camouflaged all the tears she'd shed during the last forty-eight hours. After Mike died, she hadn't thought she'd ever cry so much again. Or feel so bereft. But she couldn't have been more wrong. Her heart ached as if it had been shredded into millions of tiny bits.

So far, the singular plus in her week was Dwayne's conspicuous absence. Except for giving her a few crisp instructions, he'd made himself scarce.

Out of the corner of her eye, Joanna caught Darlene observing her from the doorway. Quickly, she swiveled in her chair and flipped on the power button to her computer printer.

"You look terrible," her co-worker commented as she laid a sheaf of papers on the orderly desk.

"I feel terrible." Joanna blew her nose into a damp Kleenex.

"If I were in that bad shape, I'd take the day off. And the day after that. Maybe a whole week."

"I can't afford the time. I have to update the latest marketing figures for the entire northeastern region." She sniffed. "By tomorrow afternoon."

"Tell Simmons to stuff it."

"No way." Joanna wasn't asking any more favors of Dwayne. "I'll—" A sneeze cut off her remark.

"All right. Go ahead and play the martyr. What kind of flowers should I order for your funeral?" At the look of despair that crossed Joanna's face, Darlene backed off. "Sorry, that wasn't kind. But is the future of Wilkins' worth chancing a bout with pneumonia?"

"I don't have pneumonia."

"Not yet, maybe, but you're headed for it. Can I get you something? Aspirin? A cup of hot tea . . . ? A shot of whiskey?"

Joanna managed a tepid smile. "Afraid not. I've already had my quota of aspirin for the day, and I've drunk so much hot liquid, my insides feel like a beach at high tide. The whiskey is tempting, but I don't think management would approve."

Darlene wiggled her eyebrows. "I'd never tell."

"You wouldn't have to. In my present state, one slug would be enough to knock me out."

"Might not be a bad idea." Darlene headed for the door. "Well, if you need anything, give a yell."

"Thanks, I will." Joanna turned back to the computer screen and entered a command to print out the first set of figures.

An image of Scott instantly filled her mind, and she no longer had the strength to push it aside. Unconsciously she swept her tongue over her lips in memory of his parting kiss. Could she call what she was feeling for him love?

No, she told herself emphatically. Nor would she be fooled into loving a second time.

Joanna forced her attention back to her assignment. She watched as the printer spewed forth page after page of statistics. Her skull felt as if a weight were pressing down on it, but it wasn't the printer's ceaseless regurgitation of material that was giving her a headache. It was a sudden moment of clarity, a flash of insight. Despite a valiant attempt to guard her emotions, she had failed. Whether she wanted to or not, she'd once again lost her heart. Lost it completely and irrevocably to Scott.

Moisture gathered at the corners of her eyes, and she plucked a clean tissue from her nearly depleted box. Scott had called her a coward, and rightly so. Tears trickled down her cheeks. Tears of remorse. Tears of yearning. Tears of futility.

What, she lamented, was she going to do now?

* * *

"Hurry up, Mom! We're going to be late!" Tony pleaded.

"I'm working as fast as I can." Joanna was whipping the chocolate icing for her devil's food cake. "Go read a book. Watch TV. Anything. You're making me nervous."

"Okay," Tony grumped, reluctantly stomping out of the kitchen.

With her wrist, Joanna pushed a lock of hair away from her eyes. Before she'd come down with her cold—and before her break-up with Scott—she'd promised Beverly, who was in charge of organizing the school district's annual fall carnival, that she'd bake a cake for the event. And not just any cake, but Mike's favorite—the Mansfield Chocolate Overdose. When they'd married, he'd made certain Joanna's mother gave her a copy of the recipe, which had been in the family for generations.

Once, Joanna had made the mistake of telling Beverly about it, and her bouncy neighbor had insisted that she contribute the pièce de résistance to the carnival—which was the district's biggest moneymaker for supporting extracurricular activities, like the One-for-One Club.

"The Chocolate Overdose is bound to sell tons of tickets for the cake walk!" her neighbor had enthused.

Joanna didn't resent the none-too-subtle arm twisting. Normally she took pleasure in creating the rich dessert, though it required more care—and time—than most cakes. But today was different. For one thing, she was still running a low-grade fever and didn't feel up to the extra effort. More to the point, she didn't want to go to the carnival at all. With her luck, she was bound to run into Scott, and after their argument, she wasn't ready to face him again.

Joanna swirled the last spoonful of icing onto the cake. And not a second too soon, because Tony was once again hopping from foot to foot at the door. "Aren't you finished yet?" he complained, unable to disguise his restlessness.

"As we speak, ta-dah—the final stroke." She picked up the cake on its heavy cardboard base for his inspection. "How does it look?"

Tony smacked his lips. "I'm gonna buy a ticket for the cake walk. I hope I win it."

"If you don't, I'll bake another."

"Tomorrow?"

Joanna laughed. "Give me a few days to recuperate! I could fix a five-course dinner in the same time it takes me to put together one of these." Carefully, she eased the six-inch-high concoction into the large box she'd purchased at a bakery. "All set," she announced.

"All right!" Tony whooped.

For the first time ever, this year's carnival had been planned to coincide with Halloween. Beverly, in typical steamroller fashion, had pooh-poohed the notion that the kids would prefer going out trick-or-treating, arguing that they'd all be much safer coming to Whittier than running around on the streets.

Over the objections of some of the other committee members, Beverly had won out. She'd assured everyone that young and old alike would love it, and if attendance at the event was any measure of success, she'd been right. Joanna tried to find a parking space close to the school but had to settle for a spot two blocks away.

"How do I look?" Tony asked, referring to his medieval squire's outfit.

"Terrific!"

"I'd rather have come as a knight."

"I know, darling, but hammering out a suit of armor for you would have been a bit difficult," she noted dryly.

"You don't think I look silly?"

"How can you look silly? You're in costume. All the kids will be."

"They're giving prizes, you know."

"No, I didn't."

"For the prettiest, the most elab—elab-something."

"Elaborate?"

"Yeah, that's it, elaborate. And the differentest."

"Most different," she corrected.

"Most different," he obligingly repeated. "Stuff like that."

"You should enter."

"Which one?"

"The prettiest, of course."

"Oh, Mom, you're goofy."

"I'm teasing, sweetheart. But I definitely think you'd qualify for the most unusual."

"You've never seen anybody dressed up like me?"

"Never. Clowns, ghosts, cartoon characters, animals, pirates—you name it. But not a single squire."

"Well," Tony hedged, "maybe."

As they walked up the steps of the school, Joanna asked, "Do you have your money?"

He patted a pocket. "Uh-huh."

"Remember, I'll be manning the pie-throwing booth, so if you need me, you know where to look."

"You told me that a million times."

"And you've arranged to go around with Chris Edwards and his dad?"

Beverly had filled her in on the Edwards family. There were five children, each of whom had been a regular terror. Chris was the youngest and perhaps the worst. He was very bright, very outgoing—and constantly skirting the edge of trouble. He seemed to have a talent for judging how far he could go without someone letting him have it.

That scrap of information was enough to make Joanna clearly uneasy. After Tony's rocky start in school, the last thing he needed was an unsavory influence.

Yet she was reluctant to say anything that might interfere with the friendship. Tony seemed so happy. For the past week, he'd talked about practically nothing but his friend. Joanna thought if she heard the name Chris once more , she'd start foaming at the mouth. At the same time, she was glad for the diversion. Tony hadn't thought to ask why Scott no longer stopped by to see them.

"Yes, Mother, I'll be with Chris."

Joanna couldn't help smiling. Whenever Tony called her "Mother," she knew he was near the end of his rope, and so she eased up. "Have a good time. If I don't run into you before, I'll meet you at ten o'clock by the trophy case." Tony didn't permit her another word before he was off and running.

To Joanna, it seemed that every student enrolled in the area schools had decided to blow off steam at the carnival. With difficulty, she threaded her way through the noisy crowd. Beverly had scheduled her into the pie-throwing booth from eight until nine, and she had a scant ten minutes before she was to relieve Claire Richards, whom she hadn't seen since the end of soccer season.

She finally made it to the booth with a few seconds to spare. "Whew! What a mob!" she announced as she let herself in through the swinging gate.

"You can say that again." Claire collected a ticket from a teenager dressed as an Indian and, in return, handed him three aluminum pie plates filled with shaving foam. She grimaced as "Eagle Eye" launched the first of his missiles at the face peering out through a hole in the sheet. "I pity some of the teachers who volunteer. The kids line up by the dozens to get in a few licks at the most unpopular ones. We try to keep the schedule secret, but somehow they always find out when Mr. Obnoxious or Ms. Intolerable is playing target."

Joanna squeezed her eyes shut as the last of the plates landed a bull's-eye. "Must be a popular booth."

"That it is. A terrific moneymaker." Claire called to the volunteer who was wiping his face clean as best he could. "You'll be happy to hear, Mr. Billings, that your time's up. Our replacements have arrived."

The man's expression of gratitude said more than words possibly could. Briefly a gaping hole appeared in the middle of the sheet before a fresh face—this time a woman's—poked its way through.

"I suppose Beverly told you what to do."

Joanna laughed. "Right down to the color of the tickets."

"Have fun, then," Claire remarked with a departing wave. "I'm off to track down Shelly."

To Joanna's amazement the next hour seemed to fly by. She suspected, however, that the hands of the clock dragged for the teachers, although their tour of duty ran only fifteen minutes.

Between collecting tickets, filling pie tins and helping as best she could to clean faces, she felt as if she were working on an assembly line. Joanna's hands could barely move fast enough. At one point, several high schoolers, who'd lined up to take aim at their history teacher, Miss Hawk, gave Joanna a lot of flak. But she considered herself lucky—better a few verbal barbs than a face full of shaving cream.

She could hardly believe it when someone gently tapped her on the shoulder. "Okay, dearie, I'm to take over," a woman, who was eighty if she was a day, announced.

Joanna consulted her watch. Sure enough, it was a couple of minutes before nine. Without so much as a by your leave, the octogenarian took the aerosol can from Joanna's hand and started filling pans. "Come one, come all," she bellowed above the noise. "One ticket entitles you to three shots at your favorite teacher!"

A smile tilted the corners of Joanna's mouth. Obviously the elderly woman was an old hand helping out at carnival time.

Slipping through the gate, she decided to browse for a while, keeping one eye out for Tony, the other for Scott. The former she wanted to see, the latter to avoid.

She passed a group of younger students bobbing for apples and skirted the line waiting to get into the haunted house. At one of the booths, she noticed that Abby Wilson was up to her usual tricks, trying to entice the male half of the species with her kind of Halloween treat. Clad in a red bikini, which, in Joanna's estimation, stopped just short of being indecent, she sat perched at the end of a diving board, giggling as men, who should be old enough to know better, threw baseballs at a metal plate. A solid hit and Abby was dunked in a vat of water. The number of males lined up attested to the woman's popularity. Her booth would undoubtedly add quite a few dollars to the district's activity fund.

With a snort of distaste, Joanna walked on. Just as she was making her way past a colorful tent, she heard a heavily accented voice call, "Mrs. Parker."

She turned one way, then the other, but could locate no familiar face. "Mrs. Parker," the voice hissed again. This time Joanna faced the tent. Sitting before a crystal ball was none other than the professed witch of Decatur Street.

"Well, if it isn't—" Joanna cleared her throat, trying for a natural voice "—Hecate."

"Madam Skyah," the woman corrected. "Tonight, as you see, I wear my Halloween costume."

For the first time Joanna noticed the gypsy garb and made a concerted effort not to smile. Did the eccentric woman really think she had to dress up for Halloween?

With a toothy grin, Madam Skyah waved her hand at the painted sign above the entrance. "Come. Let me tell your fortune."

Joanna, who knew that she was more superstitious than any modern-thinking person ought to be, shrugged. "I...uh...didn't buy any tickets."

The smile remained in place. "No matter. It's on the house. You'll help draw more customers."

Covertly Joanna glanced around her, hoping no one she knew would see her duck into the old lady's tent.

Madam Skyah held out a bony hand and accepted Joanna's palm. For endless minutes she studied the lines as intently as if they were roads on a map that would lead to Bluebeard's treasure. At last, in an unearthly voice she droned, "I see a happy future for you. Look at this." Her index finger traced a line along Joanna's palm. "It shows you're going to have a long life. Ah, and romance. Romance," she announced gleefully, "is going to be important. Look here. See how sharply etched these two grooves are? Especially this one. That means you'll have two great loves in your life, the second—" she winked suggestively "—more significant than the first."

The prediction hit Joanna with the force of a sledgehammer. Could this self-appointed seer be right? Impossible! And yet...

When the woman who now called herself Madam Skyah frowned, Joanna realized a moment of panic. "What's wrong?" she asked.

"Nothing, nothing. I was counting these lines here."

Joanna lowered her head and peered intently. "Why?"

"They tell me how many children you'll have."

Intrigued, Joanna inquired, "And how many have you found?"

"Twelve."

"Twelve!"

At that moment a deep voice from behind her inserted, "Isn't it time you got started on the next eleven?"

Joanna swung around, her eyes colliding with Scott's. One hand held an extra-tall cake box; the other rested on Tony's shoulder.

The boy's eyes were wide with amazement. "I'm gonna have some brothers and sisters like Chris?" The surprise turned to joy as he launched himself at his mother. "Yippee!"

Color suffused Joanna's cheeks. With Tony's arms hugging her in a death grip, she stumbled to her feet.

"That'll be better than a dog. Or Miss Kitty!" he hooted, then looked at Scott. "Well, almost."

"Tony," Joanna said in a voice she prayed sounded light, "I don't think you should get your hopes up."

"But this lady said you'd have a bunch of kids."

"She doesn't really know the future, dear. She's guessing."

Tony cocked his head. "Then why did you listen to her?"

"I—I," Joanna stammered, not knowing how to refute her son's logic. "I was merely having some fun." She could feel one pair of eyes boring into her back, the other into her front. "You never told me you felt deprived because you didn't have brothers and sisters."

"What's *deprived* mean?"

"That you want something you don't have."

"I didn't feel . . . what did you call it? De—de-pried. Until I heard what that lady said." He directed a finger at the old woman, and reflexively Joanna nudged his hand to his side. "If I had brothers and sisters, I'd always have somebody to play with. Wouldn't I?"

Embarrassed at the direction the conversation was taking in front of Scott, Joanna tried for an indulgent smile and asked if Tony had any tickets left. When he handed her three, she gave one to Madam Skyah. "I insist," she said somewhat formally. "Thank you for reading my palm."

Scott offered the woman a grin. "She'll keep you posted on the results."

Joanna took Tony's hand and led him away from the tent. "Did you and Chris have a good time?"

"The best! Chris won a stuffed animal at the baseball-throwing booth. I tried, but I didn't hit enough bottles." His face brightened. "I did get fourth prize for my costume."

"I knew it. In the most unusual category?"

"Nope."

"What then?"

"The funniest."

Joanna's brow creased. "Why did you enter that division?"

"'Cause when Chris saw me, he busted out laughing."

"He did, did he?" Joanna was a bit miffed. She'd spent a lot of time putting Tony's costume together. "What did he find so funny?"

"My wig. He thought I looked like a girl."

"That's the way men wore their hair during the Middle Ages. Did that upset you?" she asked cautiously.

"Nah. His costume was a lot weirder'n mine. He was a ghost."

"What's so strange about that?"

"His mom used an old sheet." He put his hand over his mouth to stifle a giggle. "It had great big red flowers on it."

In spite of herself, Joanna began to chuckle. "I take it he got first place for the funniest?"

"No, second. But not for the funniest." Like a comedian delivering the punch line, he paused before revealing, "For the prettiest!"

Joanna shook her head. "I'm not going to pursue that. You have two tickets left, Tony. Go on and use them before we start home."

"Okay. I'll give one to the clown with prizes in his pockets. After that—" he nodded toward Abby Wilson "—I'm gonna try to dunk her."

All the time they'd been talking, Scott had followed along in their wake. Though Joanna had tried to ignore him, she was painfully aware of his presence.

When Tony dashed off to cash in his last two tickets, Scott fell in step beside her. "Beverly's done a great job, hasn't she?"

"I can't say I'm surprised," Joanna allowed. "She's some organizer. And she has a way of corralling volunteers."

"If she's not careful, she'll get stuck with the job again next year."

"I have a feeling she wouldn't mind." Joanna angled him a genuine smile. "I see you won something tonight."

"A cake."

"The box looks familiar."

"It should. You baked it."

What a coincidence, she thought, that Scott should win her cake. Pondering what significance Hecate, alias Madam Skyah, would read into that, she nearly missed his next comment.

"I'm going to share it with someone special."

Joanna was crestfallen. Some other woman would be eating *her* cake. Suddenly she saw red. "Well," she declared acidly, "don't let me hold you up."

"Don't worry. You're not. I'm waiting for Tony."

"Can't you see him at school?"

"Sure, but I promised him some of your cake. He's not going to like it if I take off without giving him a chunk."

"Tony?"

At her confused stare, he repeated, "Yes, Tony. That cute little fellow over there throwing baseballs? Your son?"

Joanna's relief was practically tangible, but she'd die before she let on. "You don't have to," she sniffed. "I can bake another one."

"According to him, that's easier said than done. He informed me that you slaved over this cake for days."

"He was exaggerating. It was more like hours."

"The point is, why go to so much trouble again? After all, it's too big a cake for one person."

"Mom!" Tony interrupted. "Did you see that?"

Somewhat disoriented, she whirled in the direction of her son's voice. "See what?"

"That!" He pointed toward the tank where Abby was hauling herself out of the water. "I did it. They gave me three balls and the third time I hit the target and down she went. Splash!" he waved his arms in a huge circle to emphasize what had taken place.

"Congratulations," she said, discovering Abby's eyes on the three of them.

"I was telling your mother," Scott put in, "that you'd like some of her cake."

"Yeah, Mom. What'd'ya say we go home and have a piece?"

"It's getting late, Tony," Joanna evaded.

Scott glanced at his watch. "Come on, Jo. It's Saturday night. No one has to get up early in the morning. Besides it's Halloween. And this is an extraordinary dessert."

"That's right, Mom. Please?"

She glanced from the man to the boy. The beseeching look on her son's face would have melted the heart of the most hardened criminal. And whenever Scott called her Jo, he struck a responsive chord.

"One piece," she emphasized, "then off to bed you go."

Scott put his empty plate on the coffee table. "That, without a doubt, is the best cake I've ever tasted. And the richest."

"Can I have another slice, Mom?"

"Absolutely not. Scott's taking the rest home. One more bite of chocolate on top of all the other stuff you ate at the carnival, and you'll end up sick."

"You always say that," he groused, "and I never do. Anyhow, Coach said he'd leave me some more."

"Then you can save it for tomorrow."

"Do I have to take a bath?"

"Yes. That makeup might stain your sheets."

"Do I have to brush my teeth?"

"Not if don't mind losing them."

"Then I wouldn't hav'ta brush 'em."

Scott rumpled the boy's hair. "You wouldn't be able to eat your favorite foods, either. Like pizza. Did you think about that?"

"I guess not."

"They why don't you stop giving your mother a hard time?" Though the question was couched in a voice that was gentle, it brooked no argument.

"Yes, sir." Without rancor, Tony took off for the bathroom.

"I wish I had your air of authority." Joanna tilted her head. "Maybe that's not the right word. What I'm trying to say is you have an uncanny ability to get Tony to do what you want without his balking...or without making him mad at you."

Scott chuckled. "Principals get lots of practice."

"No, it's more than that. I've had six years experience as a mother, and I seldom meet with your success. It's a special gift."

"Wait until you have those eleven other children," he teased. "Not that I don't appreciate the compliment. You were complimenting me, weren't you?"

"Of course." She paused before adding, "I want to thank you for all you've done for Tony, Scott."

He leaned forward. "Joanna, I—I'm sorry I walked out on you the other night. This past week has been hell."

He was so sincere, so earnest, Joanna could feel her defenses crumble. "For me, too," she replied honestly.

Scott slid out of his chair to sit beside her on the sofa. "I care about you, Jo. Would you mind if...we gave it another try? Could we start over?"

The slight hesitancy in his voice tugged at her heart. She had no strength left, no desire even to fight her emotions. Tenderly, she reached up and touched his face. "Okay, but no promises."

"Fair enough." Shuddering, he gathered her in his arms and lowered his mouth to hers. The kiss was filled with restrained passion. Warmth curled deep inside Joanna, and she ran her fingers through his hair.

Scott angled his head to deepen the kiss when Joanna became aware of a silence from the bathroom. Reluctantly, she pulled herself from his arms. Before she had a chance to think about it, she whispered, "Tony's spending tomorrow night at Chris's. Would you like to come to dinner?"

Scott's grin was wolfish. "That's the best invitation I've been issued in a long time."

As she examined her words, her face reddened in embarrassment. "I didn't mean—"

He nuzzled her throat. "I know you didn't. We'll take it a step at a time."

When he heard the bathroom door open, Scott drew back. "Until tomorrow night," he murmured, grazing a knuckle down her cheek. "I'll supply dessert."

Good Lord, Joanna silently wailed. What had she gotten herself into? Her lips parted, but mesmerized by his gaze, she could summon no protest.

Chapter Ten

"**O**uch!" Joanna squeaked when she accidentally brushed her index finger against the oven rack. Dropping the hot pads, she stuck her finger in her mouth, then flipped on the water, letting it run until it was cold enough to take the sting out of the burn.

Scott poked his head through the door. "You okay?"

Joanna pulled her hand out from under the cold water and waggled her finger. "A little burn."

"I'll get you some ice." Scott moved toward the refrigerator. The next thing Joanna knew, he'd taken her hand in his and was running a cube over the pinkened flesh.

As always his touch set off something warm inside her. Joanna longed to plow her free fingers into his thick wavy hair, trace a knuckle over his firm jaw, clasp a hand around his wide shoulder. She felt her knees go weak.

"Better?" Scott asked, giving her a smile that sent a shaft of awareness directly to her midsection. His fingertips followed the ice, alternately chilling and warming her skin.

"Better," she mumbled, though by this time she wasn't certain what was supposed to be better.

"To be on the safe side, maybe I should kiss it." Scott tossed the cube in the sink and brought her hand to his mouth, lightly touching his lips to her finger. "Umm, you taste good." With exquisite slowness, he nibbled his way over her wrist and up her arm, not stopping until he reached her slender neck.

Afterward, Joanna couldn't have told anyone how it happened, but the next instant she found herself sandwiched between the refrigerator and Scott's firm body. The naked longing in his eyes held her spellbound as his head lowered and his mouth claimed hers.

Scott's lips played havoc with her senses. The kiss began softly, almost teasingly, but rapidly turned greedy. Though Joanna's subconscious warned her that she was flirting with danger, she refused to heed it. She ignored her uncertainty about a long-term commitment. She spared no thought for her fears about the future. She was too caught up in a flood of delicious sensations to allow negative feelings to intrude.

With all her emotions focused on Scott, she locked her arms around his waist and opened her mouth to his invading tongue.

Scott knew the exact moment he'd won the battle. Joanna's pliant body couldn't seem to press close enough. It was as if she were trying to burrow right into his skin. Her hands chased with abandon up and down his back. When his lips left hers to scatter kisses along the delicate line of her jaw, she whimpered helplessly and arched her neck to give him better access.

Her ready response was unbearably exciting. He could feel his heart thundering in his chest, his blood surging thickly through his veins. He wanted to lose himself in her taste, her scent, her softness. His lips played with the small lobes of her ears and skimmed warmly over her cheeks. "God, but you're sweet," he murmured, the words hot and moist against her skin. Framing her face, he brought her mouth back to his for another long, draining kiss.

Joanna went weightless, awash with a tide of desire. She loved the feel of him, the taste of him. Freeing his shirt, she let her fingers find the bare flesh beneath. Their tips glided over hard muscle, crisp chest hair, heated skin. She wanted to linger over each new texture, but she couldn't seem to still her restless fingers. Like a woman driven, she had to chart each rugged sinew, every hardened inch of his muscled length.

Her impatience drew a long groan from Scott. Cupping her bottom, he ground his hips against her, letting her know how much her urgency inflamed him. He tore his mouth from hers only long enough to pull the sweater she wore over her head. To his delight, she hadn't bothered with a bra. He seriously doubted he could rule his trembling fingers well enough to deal with tiny clasps.

He tried to put the brakes on their rapidly escalating desire, but Joanna was making it impossible for him to hold back. With one hand she plucked at the buttons of his shirt while the other worked on his belt buckle. The scrape of her nails on his bare skin, the flutter of her thick lashes against his cheek, the alluring scent of her cologne were incredibly arousing. Without stopping to ask her permission, he scooped her into his arms and headed for the bedroom.

In a single motion he laid her on the satiny spread, then came down beside her. Raw need knifed through him as his mouth laid greedy claim to her breasts. When a harsh moan issued from deep within Joanna's throat, he hastily peeled off their remaining clothing. Out of the corner of his eye, he caught the glint of a gold picture frame sitting on the nightstand. He leaned over and placed it facedown, then positioned himself over her.

"Look at me, Jo."

"I can't," she whispered. "I don't have the strength to open my eyes."

"Look at me!" he ordered, this time more harshly.

Slowly her lids fluttered open. "Why?"

"Because I want you to know who's making love to you."

Little by little Joanna regained consciousness to find herself sheltered in Scott's strong arms. He was brushing long strands of hair away from her cheeks, examining her face as closely as a scientist does a specimen beneath his microscope.

At the smile that automatically curved her mouth, the lines of strain furrowing his brow disappeared. "I'm sorry I hurt you."

"You didn't," she insisted, though she couldn't disguise a wince when she shifted her lower body slightly.

"Yes, I did." His voice was laced with self-accusation. In the soft lamp light, he continued his close scrutiny. "I was an animal."

"I didn't exactly kick and scream and try to beat you off." Joanna gave a throaty laugh. "You've always seemed so incredibly patient. I rather liked making you wild," she said smugly. "It made me feel very... feminine... powerful."

"Oh, yeah?"

She trailed a finger across his jaw. "Yeah."

"Think you're pretty clever, don't you? Suppose you can do it again? Cause me to lose control?" There was amusement in his eyes, but also hunger—and challenge.

"Uh-huh. And this time I'll go one better. I'll teach you how it's done." Pushing him to the mattress, she lowered her mouth to his.

Scott gave her scant opportunity to make good on the promise. When her lips moved down his throat and began to spread wet kisses over his chest, he took the initiative and rolled her onto her back. This time the loving was slow and gentle and tender. He ranged over her body with the thoroughness of an early explorer, leaving not a single inch unexamined, untouched.

By the time he joined them together, Joanna was the one who'd been taught a lesson about losing control.

"Their skin looks a little like Tony's after he's spent an hour playing around in his bath water." Joanna was referring to the shriveled potatoes and carrots lying at the bottom of the roasting pan. "And this—" she nudged the English cut of beef with a fork "—isn't fit for a dog."

"I guess I owe you another apology."

"For what?"

"Ruining your dinner."

"It's no big deal. But I'm not sure what I'm going to feed you."

Scott took her in his arms and nuzzled her neck. "You already satisfied my appetite. The only thing I was hungry for was you, Jo."

"Flatterer! But, as the saying goes, you can't live on love."

"I'm willing to give it a try."

"You have a one-track mind, Scott Hartman!" she scolded, but softened the complaint by caressing him with her eyes.

His heart soared. "I wouldn't object to sacrificing a few pounds in the cause of love."

"I wouldn't want you wasting away on my account. I like you too much the way you are." She slipped from his embrace and went to the refrigerator. Pulling open the door, she rummaged through the contents. "Do you object to leftovers?"

"Lady, I'll take your leftovers any day."

Joanna laughed and warded off another advance with uplifted palms. "You won't have the strength if you don't let me feed you first."

They made do with sandwiches, chips and a Jell-o salad. When they'd finished, Joanna started to stack their dirty dishes, but Scott reached out a hand and banded her wrist. "Those can wait—this can't."

At the seriousness in his voice, Joanna's heart practically stopped beating, then took off at a gallop. "What can't wait?"

He pulled her onto his lap. "What I've been aching to say for weeks. I love you, Jo."

Joanna tried to speak but had trouble locating her voice. "Scott . . . I—I didn't engineer our lovemaking. I invited you to dinner—as a simple thank-you for all your kindnesses. I planned a plain, ordinary meal—pot roast. Nothing romantic—no candlelight, no flowers, no music." She looked down at her baggy sweater and jeans. "And I obviously didn't dress with seduction in mind. It was something that just happened." She gave a short laugh. "I'm all grown-up. I don't expect declarations of love in return for—"

"Sleeping with me?" he finished for her. "Damn it, Joanna, do you think what went on in your bedroom was nothing but a roll in the hay?" When she didn't respond, he dropped her hand.

She slipped off his lap and grabbed up the stack of dirty dishes. "I know what you're thinking," she protested, moving toward the sink, "but you're wrong. It was more than sex."

"Really?" he said coldly.

"Scott, you have to understand. It's been a long time…. Other than Mike, you're the only man I've…" Turning, she braced her back against the counter.

"I get your drift. You haven't been with anyone else since your husband died." His eyes pinned hers. "Oh, yes, I saw his picture by your bed. You don't have to tell me. He's the only man you ever loved. So you've decided to dedicate the rest of your life to his memory. Only tonight your physical needs got the best of you. After all, it's well over two years. Right?"

"Scott, that's not—"

"Don't say anything." He shoved his chair back with such force it nearly toppled over. "You're a passionate woman, Joanna. You sure as hell proved that tonight. And now that your passions have been reawakened, I expect it'll be impossible for you to remain celibate another two years. But I won't provide stud service. I'm sure your old boss—what's his name? Simmons?—would be more than happy to oblige." He sprang to his feet. "When I walked out of here before, I should have kept on going." His fist slammed onto the table, rattling the few remaining dishes. "This time, by damn, I will."

Joanna covered her face with her hands. For the second time in the space of hours, the unflappable Scott Hartman was losing control. His anger was so out of character that instead of being upset, she was amused. Bending over double, she fought an unreasonable urge to burst out laughing. The effort caused a flood of tears to stream down her cheeks.

Taken aback by her distress, Scott yearned to go to her, pull her in his arms and offer her comfort. But he questioned the wisdom of such a move and stood helplessly by until the spasms ceased. When they were replaced by huge gulps of air, he ventured, "Jo—"

Before he could finish, Joanna straightened, lowered her hands and . . . giggled.

Scott's jaw sagged. "What the hell? I thought you were crying."

"No," she sputtered. "Laughing."

"My mistake." He whirled on a heel and tried to push past her, but she raised her arms to block his exit. "I can explain."

"No explanations are necessary. I may not be as smart as . . ." Unable to bring himself to say Mike, he tacked on, "I'm no dunce, Jo."

"Who said you were?" Her gaze met his. "You know how I envy your patience. Well, you've blown your image tonight. Not once, but twice." She offered him a smile. "That's why I couldn't help myself. It was such fun watching you lose your cool."

Joanna waited for a response. When none came, she suddenly grew serious. Tonight had confirmed her deep feelings for Scott. Though their lovemaking had come about more through accident than design, Joanna knew that if she weren't emotionally involved, they'd never have ended up in bed. Casual sex had never held any appeal for her.

Moments ago Scott had said he loved her. Should she take the plunge? Should she tell him that he wasn't alone? That she returned his feelings?

Joanna felt as if she were standing at the edge of a very steep cliff. Moving a fraction of an inch forward or backward would forever alter her life.

Conscious choice was taken out of her hands when Scott again tried to step around her. Without thinking, she threw her arms around his neck. "Blast it, Scott! I love you, too."

He jerked—as if a dentist had just struck a nerve. "What did you say?"

"I love you," she repeated more forcefully than before. "I love you."

Scott couldn't believe what he was hearing. "You mean that?"

"I never meant anything more in my life."

The strain seemed to leave his body on a long, heavy sigh. "Then there's only one thing to do," he announced, pulling her into his arms.

"What's that?"

"Get married."

"Hold on, darling. Let's not rush things. You promised to go slow."

"That was yesterday."

Joanna leaned away and looked into his eyes. "I know, but I never expected to fall in love again. It's all so new. I'm having a hard enough time coming to grips with—"

"We're getting married," he repeated. "I'll have none of this coming-to-grips garbage."

His stern expression brought another bubble of laughter from Joanna. "This has been some night! I'm certainly being introduced to different facets of your personality.'' At his perplexed scowl, she explained, ''You have a much shorter fuse than I thought. As well as an alarming tendency to be domineering. What happened to all that tact and finesse?''

''I ran out of those commodities hours ago.'' He drew her close and rested his chin on the crown of her head. ''I'll let you choose the date, though. So long as it's before Christmas. We can use the following week for a honeymoon.''

''You, sir, may have time off over the holidays— being in education and all—but the rest of us peons have to work.''

''Surely Wilkins' will give you some personal days.''

''When I've only been there a few months? Fat chance.''

''Then quit.''

She backed out of his embrace enough to stare him in the eye. ''Absolutely not!''

''Okay, okay. Don't get all huffy.''

''Look who's talking!''

''So we'll compromise. We'll get married before Christmas and take a honeymoon whenever you qualify for vacation time.''

''I don't believe this conversation.''

''This isn't a conversation. It's a marriage proposal.''

''I see. Then I guess I have a choice to make.''

He shook his head in firm denial. ''I won't take no for an answer.''

''You're pressuring me again.''

He grinned at her, a gleam lighting his hazel eyes and making them dance. "Then maybe I had better dig deep and find a little bit of that patience and tact and finesse you say I'm so famous for." Slowly his mouth lowered to settle over hers.

"I'd like a small wedding," Joanna remarked the following morning over breakfast.

"That's entirely your decision, sweetheart. I don't care if we have two or two thousand in attendance."

"Just family and close friends."

"Fine," Scott agreed, finishing off his orange juice. "Speaking of family, I want you to meet mine. I'll give them a call and see if it's okay for us to go down this weekend."

Joanna's face paled. "I hope they like me," she said nervously, remembering how Mike's parents had reacted to her.

Scott reached across the table and covered her hand with his. "What's not to like? They'll love you. They're going to be so pleased to claim you as a daughter-in-law."

"The Parkers weren't thrilled," she let slip.

Scott stiffened, but managed to beat down the jealousy that always swamped him at any reference to her dead husband. "You didn't get along with them?"

"That's putting it charitably." Joanna worried her bottom lip. "It was apparent right from the beginning that they didn't approve of me. Even though I was going to college, I came from a blue-collar background. Before he retired, my father drove a bus. While the Parkers weren't wealthy, they were professionals. Mr. Parker's a pharmacist and Mrs. Parker's a legal assistant.''

"You call them Mr. and Mrs.?'' Scott was aghast.

"After Mike and I were married, I once tried to loosen up and refer to them by their first names. The atmosphere became so frosty I swear I could see my breath."

"I find it hard to believe they didn't accept you."

"No woman would ever have been good enough for their son, except maybe Florence Nightingale, Mother Teresa and Joan of Arc rolled into one. For years they'd had these grand designs for Mike's life. He was brilliant. He could have gone into a dozen different fields and risen to the top in any one, but he chose computer science. With their blessing, of course. Mike was their fair-haired boy. He had always known what he wanted out of life, and his plans never failed to meet with the approval of his parents. Until I came along. No doubt, they thought his goals were going down the drain.'' A pensive expression crossed her face. "Quite frankly, I don't know what he ever saw in me."

"I imagine he saw what I see,'' Scott said, feeling for the first time an odd sort of kinship with his nemesis. "Integrity, loyalty, warmth, intelligence...strength. And beauty. Incredible beauty. You're one classy lady, Jo.''

Embarrassed by his praise, Joanna countered, "The Parkers would take issue with that. When they found out Tony was on the way, they had a fit. A wife was a big enough drag on their son's career. But a family!''

Her features hardened. "I could forgive them for not liking me. But shunning Tony. That I'll never forget."

Scott was shocked by Joanna's revelations. "They don't love their own grandchild?"

Joanna shook her head. "They'd pinned all their hopes on Mike, and when he disappointed them, that was it." She fiddled with her coffee cup. "I thought they'd unbend a little after Tony was born. But they never did. I suppose they're put off because, unlike Mike, he's no budding genius. He's just a sweet, average kid. Apparently that's not good enough.

"Oh, sure, they occasionally mail him presents. But strictly out of duty. For his birthday, they sent him a designer jogging suit. It arrived a week late—and was too small." Her voice broke. "I could easily count on the fingers of one hand the times they've seen him since Mike's funeral."

Scott gave her arm a squeeze. "There is a bright side. The Parkers aren't likely to put up a fuss if I adopt Tony. I want to be legally responsible for him. Would you like that, Jo?"

Tears of happiness pressed behind her lids. "I'd be very pleased."

"What's more, I'd like to give him my name. With the divorce rate what it is, I see a lot of students at school who feel they don't belong. I want Tony to think of himself as a real part of our family. And I believe he's more likely to feel that way if the three of us share the same last name. But if you're a Hartman and he's a Parker..." Scott's words trailed off as if a thought had just occurred to him. "You are going to take my name, aren't you?"

The question startled Joanna. "You have to ask? As *traditional* as I am?"

"You make it sound like a dirty word! I happen to find your old-fashioned qualities endearing." He grinned. "Still, I didn't think I should take too much for granted."

Deeply touched, Joanna came around the table and slid onto Scott's lap. "Whatever did I do to deserve you?"

"I could ask the same question." Gathering her close, he tucked her head against the hollow of his shoulder.

Joanna closed her eyes. With his strong arms around her, she felt content, secure. How long had it been since she was this happy?

All at once an involuntary shudder seized her.

"You cold?" Scott asked, bundling her closer.

"Scared," she whispered.

"Of what?"

"Loving you so much." She raised her head to peer into his eyes. "I loved Mike, but it was never like this. Never this . . . this intense. I wonder how long happiness like ours can possibly last."

Scott's heart swelled until he thought it would surely burst. "Forever."

He sealed his vow with a kiss.

Chapter Eleven

"What's that?" Tony could only stare as Scott carefully maneuvered his car around a black buggy swaying to the movement of the trotting horse that pulled it along the road.

"An Amish family," Scott remarked. "They're members of a religious group. A sizeable number live here in Lancaster County."

"Why are they dressed funny? Are they too poor to buy a car?"

"They're not dressed funny—just differently," Joanna inserted. "And they're traveling by horse and buggy because they don't believe in automobiles." Though her knowledge was limited, she did know that much about the community.

"They don't?" Tony was clearly shocked.

"Nor," Scott added, "in stoves or refrigerators or computers or telephones, among other things. The Amish like to live simply. It makes them feel closer to God." He indicated a house set back a distance from the two-lane highway. "See that farm? I'm sure it belongs to an Amish family."

"How do you know?"

"Because there're no electric wires running to the house."

Tony took a second, more careful look. "Then they can't watch TV?"

"Afraid not."

Tony turned around in his seat. "I'm glad I'm not Amish."

"Oh, I don't know," Joanna remarked. "Their kind of life has a certain appeal."

Scott grinned. "Like camping?"

"Must you remind me how inept I was at coping in the great outdoors?"

"Oh, I can think of one time you weren't so inept." His grin turned roguish.

Joanna's pulse fluttered at the memory. "That's one subject we'd better not explore just now."

"Later?" he declared, his voice a silky caress.

"Much later." She wanted to sound emphatic, but the words came out in a throaty whisper.

Good grief! Joanna thought. The electricity being generated in the car could have powered twenty Amish homes.

Surreptitiously she cast a look at Tony, but he was no longer tuned into their conversation. His attention had been diverted from the picturesque scenery to Miss Kitty, who was batting her paw at the gum wrappers he'd wadded into a ball. Unlike most cats, she wasn't the least perturbed by riding in a car. In fact, when Scott had picked them up, she'd been curled on the back seat, asleep.

Joanna realized that for Tony, this trip was just another of the many excursions they'd taken with Scott. But for her it marked a turning point in their three-way relationship; he was taking them to meet his family. While she was looking forward to the weekend, her emotions waffled between elation and apprehension.

In spite of the assurance that his mother and father would love her, Joanna was a trifle gun-shy. So she'd implored Scott not to reveal their wedding plans. If this initial visit went well, they could call his parents later. After several failed attempts to talk her out of her concern, he'd reluctantly agreed. Once that was decided, it followed that they also couldn't break the news to Tony. Joanna was as certain as a zebra has stripes that her son would be too excited to keep it to himself.

Twisting around in the car seat, Joanna saw that Tony was still concentrating on the cat's antics, oblivious to the sexual currents passing between her and Scott. She settled herself as close to the driver's side as her seat belt allowed and laid a hand on his thigh. When he gave her a tender smile, her heart turned over. Instinctively she tightened her grip, her nails digging into the soft denim of his jeans.

Scott's right hand slid down to cover Joanna's, and for a long while they drove without speaking. But the mutual touching communicated as eloquently as words the desire each was feeling and longing to express.

In good time, he remarked, "Here we are."

They pulled into a gravel lane leading to a large white frame house with a yard that was every bit as well manicured as the Amish farms they'd recently passed. Joanna was instantly taken with a suspended swing and wicker rocker on the wide front porch. Tall, narrow windows flanked the entry—two on the left, one on the right—while a symmetrical row of five more marched across the upper story. On either side of the brick steps, flower beds had been trimmed back and covered with dried leaves for the winter. Imagining their bright blooms and the added splashes of color from spring through fall, Joanna felt an immediate affinity with the Hartman family home. Indeed it seemed to be reaching out to welcome her with open arms.

"There's electricity here!" Tony piped up gleefully, pointing a finger at lines leading from wooden poles to the house.

Joanna smiled at her son's joy, but she knew he wasn't thinking of the conveniences of light or central heating. His satisfaction was firmly rooted in the knowledge that he wouldn't be deprived of TV for an entire weekend.

Soon, though, her pleasure in the simplicity of the house's design and her amusement over Tony's observation gave way to nerves. What would Scott's parents really think of her?

Joanna practically jumped out of her skin when Scott curled his fingers around her arm and squeezed reassuringly. Swallowing, she schooled her features into a tepid smile.

Scott parked alongside a late-model station wagon and a rusted-out van, then cut the engine. "Looks like the folks are having a family reunion." He hiked his chin toward the adjacent vehicles. "Those belong to my sister and brother."

"Great." Joanna pushed the word through taut lips.

"Is that a problem?"

"It's stupid, I know, but I can't seem to shake the impression that I'm being displayed like some champion heifer."

"I'd say more like a prize filly—all beauty and grace and energy."

Joanna experienced a tiny glow of pleasure at his compliment. Even so, the butterflies in her stomach were multiplying at an appalling rate. She turned her head toward Tony, who was again teasing the cat with his makeshift ball. "Ready?" she asked, knowing full well the question was more for herself than for him.

Twenty minutes later her nerves had calmed. Scott's parents, Catherine and John, had greeted her and Tony with genuine warmth and good cheer. The same was true of his sister Lisa, brother David and their spouses, Jeff and Ellen. Not to mention the six nieces and nephews, whose names Joanna had caught but failed to keep straight.

The main meal of the day was served at noon. Accompanying the ham and chicken were roasted potatoes, candied carrots, corn and green beans—all grown the past summer in the Hartman garden. Topping off the meal were peach and apple pies, again baked from Catherine's own storehouse of home-canned goods.

Normally, Joanna ate a light lunch, but today she treated herself to generous helpings of everything. Lethargic from the large dinner and an overriding sense of contentment, she felt at home.

At the end of the dinner, Joanna rose and began to help collect plates.

But Catherine wouldn't hear of her lifting a finger, never mind a dish. "That's my job," she insisted. "What keeps me fit in my old age. Besides, Lisa and Ellen will help today. If you insist, you can pitch in tomorrow. Scott, why don't you take Joanna to the parlor?"

"I think I'd prefer a walk," Joanna remarked. "After such a hearty dinner, I could do with some exercise."

"That's easy enough to arrange," Scott said. "Get your jacket and I'll show you the farm. Tony, would you like to come with us?"

"He'd rather stay here," Randy, one of Catherine's grandchildren, spoke up. During the course of the meal, it had been obvious that the two boys had formed an immediate attachment. "I'm gonna teach him how to play checkers."

"Checkers?" Joanna's eyes grew round with surprise. "Aren't you a little young for that game?"

Lisa smiled indulgently at her son. "He hasn't quite learned all the intricacies, but Dad here is a regular checker master and he starts all his grandchildren young. That way he's never at a loss for a partner."

John tapped his temple with a forefinger. "Smart."

"If you're sure Tony won't be any trouble." Joanna scanned the eyes of the adults.

"With six other kids under foot?" Catherine scoffed. "Who'll notice one more? You and Scott have a nice, long walk. Tony'll be fine."

On their way down the front steps, Joanna confided, "I like your parents."

Scott took her gloved hand in his. "The feeling's mutual. I can tell."

"And here I was so nervous."

They ambled down the lane, their breaths making feathery plumes on the crisp November air. "Sure you don't want to let them in on our plans?"

"I'd rather Tony be the first to hear. Why don't we tell him after we get home tomorrow. Right afterward, we'll give your folks a call."

Scott's arm slid possessively around her waist, and he molded her to his side. "I suppose I can wait that long to let the world know you're mine."

She rested her head against his shoulder. "I think Catherine and John already suspect."

"I wouldn't be surprised. Since my divorce, I've never brought a woman home."

"I'm glad. It may be selfish, but I like being the first."

During their walk, Scott showed her only a small portion of the five-hundred-acre operation. After circumnavigating one field, where winter wheat carpeted the gentle swell with green, he took her through the woods. "David and I liked to play here when we were kids. Once, we built a tree house. Right over there." He drew her beneath a magnificent oak whose solid branches stretched in horizontal layers. "If you look near the top, you can still see part of the flooring."

Joanna gazed up the sturdy trunk and through the brown leaves that still clung stubbornly to its limbs. "It must have been fun growing up on a farm."

"I liked it. But now that I'm a man, there are other amusements I enjoy more." Turning, he plowed his fingers into her hair and angled her face for his kiss.

Joanna's eyelids lowered as she was caught up in the pressure of his warm lips moving on hers. Within seconds, the kiss went from gentle to heated to demanding, drawing from her a thrilling mix of emotions. Tenderness, need, joy, excitement. She felt the rapid flicker of his tongue over her mouth to the very tips of her toes, the circular caress of his thumbs at her temples deep in the pit of her stomach. Her lungs swelled to bursting with the clean, masculine scent of him. When at long last he dragged his mouth away, Joanna's heart was pounding in her chest.

Scott's pulse matched hers. He couldn't touch her without wanting her. All of her. He was trembling when his hands bracketed her face. Peering into her eyes, he growled, "I can see this is going to turn into one hell of a weekend."

Startled by the harshness of his tone, Joanna objected, "How can you say such a thing?"

"I mean, my love, that tonight I'll be sleeping alone. And a lonely bed's a cold one."

She smiled demurely, unreasonably flattered by his confession. "Then I guess you'll have to pull up an extra quilt and practice a little control. You used to be very good at it."

"*Used to be* is right. You're much too tempting." He prodded her with a shoulder. "I suppose I'll just have to keep you at arm's length."

"Don't you dare," she objected, snuggling closer.

"You're asking for trouble."

"Good. I've developed a taste for living dangerously."

He set her apart. "What you've developed a taste for is teasing."

Suddenly grave, she took a step back. "I didn't mean to make it hard on you."

Scott's eyebrow arched. "Maybe not, but just being near you is hard on me. Let me show you." He grabbed her hand and brought it to the fly of his jeans.

Reflexively, Joanna jerked her fingers away. Mike had never been so quick to respond to her. That she had this power over Scott was heady. And a trifle unnerving. With a coolness she was far from feeling, she suggested, "I have a better idea—and a safer one. Let's continue our tour."

He heaved a sigh. "Very well. I'll show you something . . . safer."

Laughing, she took his proffered hand.

He laced his fingers with hers, and for a time they walked along a shallow brook that meandered through the farm. "During hot summers when we didn't get much rain, the stream would almost dry up, stranding hundreds of tadpoles in tiny, little puddles. Lisa used to come down and rescue every single one she could lay her fingers on."

"How...humane," Joanna said for lack of a better word.

"For the frogs they grew into, maybe. Not for the bugs they ate. She probably upset the ecological balance around here for years."

Scott showed Joanna the pond that he'd fished in summers and skated on winters, as well as the newly erected metal barn where tools, equipment and machinery were stored. Urban born and bred, Joanna marveled at the size of the tractors, the wheat combine, the corn picker.

She stepped a little closer to Scott when he introduced her to the cows—much bigger up close, she decided, than they looked when grazing in the fields. She cooed at the sheep but lifted her nose at the hogs. When Scott informed her that pigs were very intelligent animals, she turned on him a jaundiced eye.

"Really," he insisted. "They're smarter than dogs. A few years back the neighbors west of us kept one for a pet. Inside the house."

"I don't believe you."

He placed a palm over his chest. "Would I lie to you?"

"You'd enjoy giving me a hard time."

"Hmmm. A delicious idea."

"Stop distorting my words." She gave his hand a swat. "And don't think you can distract me. If you expect me to buy that pig story, you must believe I came straight off the farm."

"Careful. You're maligning my background."

"No, merely pointing out that I'm not as dumb as—"

"You look?" he finished for her.

When she jabbed him in the ribs with an elbow, he yelped.

Joanna sniffed haughtily. "Serves you right."

"Look, if you won't take my word for it, call up Homer Johnson."

"Homer Johnson?"

"Our neighbor with the pet pig." Scott once more draped his arm around her shoulders. "The Johnsons were real upset when Matilda died. She chewed through an extension cord in the basement and electrocuted herself. Fred Bryce, he's another neighbor, tried to console them. Told them to look on the bright side— they could have fresh pork chops for supper. It was two years before any of the Johnsons spoke to Fred."

Scott sounded so sincere that Joanna rolled her eyes. "If I didn't know better, I'd swear you were telling the truth."

"I am!" he insisted. "Just call Homer."

By the time they'd circled back to the Hartman house, Matilda had been long forgotten. The subject was even further buried when they encountered a minor crisis—Tony's loss of a second tooth. It had been loose for the past week, and when he'd bitten down on a crunchy apple, out it had popped.

"How will the tooth fairy know where to find me?" he wailed.

Scott swung the boy up into his arms. "Don't worry. The tooth fairy's like Santa Claus. She's one smart lady."

Tony played with the metal tab on Scott's jacket. "But when she doesn't find me at home, how will she figure out where I am?"

"Not many people know this," Scott whispered conspiratorially, "but the tooth fairy has scouts who keep track of all boys and girls with loose teeth. So no matter where one falls out, she knows about it."

"Like Santa has elves to help him?"

"Exactly. No doubt the other night one of her scouts overheard your mom and me talking about visiting my folks."

"What if I stayed with Randy? Would she look for me there?"

"Sure. Believe me, that scout's got her eye on you. Wherever you sleep tonight, the tooth fairy's bound to show up."

"But I didn't bring the box she's supposed to put my quarter in."

"I bet Lisa can find a spare one around her house. Can't you, sis?"

"No trouble."

Tony's arms flew around Scott's neck while he and Lisa exchanged a covert wink.

Tears pricked Joanna's eyes. Scott was going to make a terrific father. He had all the right instincts.

And Tony. Well, she could hardly wait until tomorrow night to give him the good news.

Though her son had never specifically told her he wanted a new daddy, his actions spoke for him. It was apparent that Tony adored Scott, who'd become more than his principal, his coach or his One-for-One friend.

Over the top of Tony's head, Scott's gaze met and held Joanna's. "If you're going to spend the night with Randy, I think I'll take your mother out to dinner."

Joanna negated his suggestion with a shake of her head. "I couldn't possibly eat another big meal today."

"Nonsense. After that exhilarating two-hour walk, you must have worked up an appetite."

She wasn't certain what he meant by "appetite." Her mouth opened, then closed. Something stirred in the region of her stomach, but it wasn't a hunger pang. The prospect of a whole evening with Scott all to herself was dizzying. Still, she protested, reminding him that she hadn't brought anything to wear except jeans and slacks since she hadn't thought they would be leaving the farm.

Scott's eyes took careful measure of her. "You're about the same size as Lisa. I'm certain she can lend you something appropriate."

And so it was decided. Tony would sleep over at Randy's; Joanna and Scott would enjoy an evening out.

"This is, without a doubt, the most romantic spot," Joanna enthused, unable to get over the quaintness of the Adrian Inn. Built of fieldstone along the banks of the Susquehanna River during the 1830s, it had played host to travelers on their way west until well after the Civil War, when it fell into decline. For a few years, it had served the area's children as a schoolhouse. Around the turn of the century, local farmers pressed it into service for grain storage. Sometime later, it was abandoned.

Then twenty years ago an enterprising New Yorker acquired the neglected property. Following the original plans, which had been preserved in the Historical Society's files, the new owner had—stone by stone— lovingly restored the inn to the glory of its early days.

"The Adrian is probably Lancaster County's most exclusive dining spot," Scott noted.

Glancing at the menu, Joanna could only agree. "The price of one dinner would keep me in groceries the rest of the month."

"Forget what's on the right side. Look at the left."

She licked her lips, unconsciously drawing his attention to their pink fullness. "In that case, I believe I'll have the Steak Diane."

Scott forced his eyes back to the menu. "Good choice. It's their specialty."

While Joanna sipped her champagne, the tuxedoed waiter expertly flambéed lean pieces of tenderloin in brandy. The flames had a mesmerizing effect. Reflected in the small-paned windows, they merged with the shafts of sunlight shimmering across the gentle waters of the Susquehanna. Joanna felt a strange peace settle over her as she watched the fiery ball slip below the horizon. No longer did she question the wisdom of falling in love with Scott. Mentally she recited a prayer of thanks that she'd found him.

After the waiter had placed artfully arranged china plates before them and unobtrusively taken his leave, Scott topped off their wine. Smiling, Joanna lifted her long-stemmed glass. "I'd like to propose a toast. To us."

"To us," Scott repeated in a husky whisper, clinking the tip of his goblet against hers.

Over dinner Joanna proclaimed the Steak Diane superb, while Scott insisted it couldn't beat his trout rolled in crushed pecans and broiled in butter. To prove his point, he lifted his fork toward her. "Here, try this."

As their eyes tangled, the lightness of their mood shifted. Scott's fork stopped midair before continuing its journey. When it reached her, Joanna's lips parted. Slowly he slipped the silver tines into her mouth and just as slowly withdrew them, his eyes never leaving hers. Mesmerized, she swallowed.

"You're right. It's m-marvelous," she stammered, suddenly nervous and excited. "Would you like a bite of mine?"

"Sweetheart, if you don't stop looking at me that way, I'll be taking lots of bites. Of Steak Joanna."

The suggestive tenor of their conversation came to a halt when the waiter appeared to claim their dishes and take their dessert order.

"Jo?" Scott inquired.

"Nothing for me, thanks."

"A brandy perhaps?"

Her eyes wandered to the silver ice bucket where the emerald-green bottle of their imported champagne sat empty. "I shouldn't," she said before relenting.

"Two brandies then."

The waiter gave a curt nod and retreated.

"Will you excuse me a minute?" Scott asked.

Joanna had just started to relax in his absence when he touched her shoulder from behind and whispered in her ear, "Come with me."

"Where?" she asked, puzzled. Once on her feet, she was a bit surprised when her head started to spin. Sitting, she'd believed the champagne had simply had a mellowing effect. Standing, she knew better. "You just ordered brandies..." she noted in her confusion."

"So I did."

She was about to tell him to cancel hers when he led her through an archway and up a flight of smoothly polished steps.

"We're having them upstairs. I've arranged for a suite."

"You did what?"

"Shhh. Let's not make a scene." He flashed an innocent smile at the descending waiter, his empty tray an indication that he'd already delivered their after-dinner drinks. Keeping a firm grip on Joanna's elbow, he quickly maneuvered her to their room.

Once he'd shut the door, she rounded on him. "What in the world made you pull a stunt like this?"

Scott shrugged boyishly. "We've both had a lot to drink. I wouldn't want to endanger us—or anyone else—by driving."

"That's..." She reached for a distinctly pungent Anglo-Saxon word, but echoes of her mother's censure prevented her from coming out with it. "That's... rubbish. You're not the least tipsy."

"This is still safer. Why are you so upset?"

"Because." She fixed her hands on her hips. "What are your parents going to think when we don't come home tonight? First, they're going to worry."

"I'm a big boy now. They no longer wait up for me."

Ignoring his easy dismissal, she went on. "When we do make an appearance, they're going to know exactly... exactly—"

"What we've been up to? If that's what bothers you, we don't have to stay all night."

"No," she said sardonically, "only long enough for a quickie. That's—"

"I thought you'd be happy with my little arrangement. After those looks you've been sending my way all evening."

"Purely your imagination," she denied.

"Liar." He moved toward her. "You've been driving me crazy. Do you have any idea what it's like to sit across from the woman you love for two hours with her nearly popping out of her dress?"

Joanna glanced down at the scooped neckline of the clingy black silk that revealed more than a hint of cleavage. "You're the one who suggested I borrow a dress from Lisa. You said we were the same size."

"You are." He grinned. "Except on top."

"I can't help the way I'm built."

"Don't get riled. It's no liability." He took another step toward her, and another, his intent clearly evident in the golden sparkle of his eyes.

Joanna held up a palm. "I have no intention of going to bed with you. If, as you say, you've had too much to drink, we'll wait until you sober up. But there's not going be a single rumple in those sheets in the next room." She tipped her head toward the door. "I will not have the help in this establishment speculating about the kind of woman I am. Checking in without luggage."

Disregarding her protests, he lightly traced a fingertip along her collarbone, down the neckline of her dress to the valley that separated her breasts. She moistened her lips and tried to inhale.

"Who cares what the help think?" Scott murmured, his breath warm against her cheek. "They don't know us from Adam. Loosen up, love. I know there's a smoldering woman beneath that proper exterior. Because I've seen her. And I'm well aware of what she does to me."

Holding her prisoner with his eyes alone, Scott tilted her forward and slowly eased down the zipper on her dress. In seconds, black silk pooled around her feet.

In a few more, Joanna's head was spinning—and not from champagne. Would Scott always have this effect on her? Would he always be able to silence her objections? She imagined so. With a single touch he could transform her into a wanton hussy.

She leaned into him, and slowly he urged her toward the canopied four-poster bed. Her concern about the inn's staff faded as he pulled her mouth to his.

Chapter Twelve

How ironic, Joanna thought as Scott pulled onto the blacktopped drive leading up to his house. She was engaged to the man, yet she'd never seen his home.

A single sweeping glance told her that she approved of his taste. Evergreens and maples surrounded the split-level, and a low autumn sun added a warm glow to the red bricks.

"I like it!" Joanna told him, and was rewarded with a pleased grin.

"Is this really your house?" Tony inquired, clearly as impressed as his mother.

"Sure is. I'll get my bag from the trunk. Why don't you carry Miss Kitty? She looks zonked. You'd think she'd driven the whole way herself."

Tony laughed and gently picked up the sleeping ball of fur. He held her close to his chest, stroking the small head that rested against his shoulder. Like a contented baby, she stretched, then went back to sleep.

"You can put her down in here," Scott told the boy. He flipped on the light in the den and indicated a large overstuffed chair. "That's where she sacks out most of the time."

His eyes swung from Tony to Joanna. "Can I get you something to eat? To drink?"

"You have root beer?" Tony asked.

"I believe so. What about you, Jo?"

"A tall glass of water—with lots of ice. Those ham sandwiches made me thirsty."

While Tony stayed in the den, downing his drink and hoping Miss Kitty would wake up so he could play with her, Scott took Joanna on a brief tour of the downstairs. He didn't know what kind of house she'd shared with Mike, but he had no illusions that he was offering her anything but a modest home. As part of the divorce settlement, he'd gotten the house, Emily the furniture. Because he hadn't bothered to replace many pieces, the place seemed Spartan.

"What do you think?" he asked anxiously, hoping Joanna wasn't too disappointed.

"I'm going to love living here," she said, making a slow circle in the middle of the living room. "It's great!"

Scott let out the breath he'd been holding. "That may be stretching a point, but I think your things will fit in nicely, don't you?"

"I'm so pleased you have room for them."

"Feel free to do what you want in the way of decoration. As you can see, I'm not much good at that sort of thing."

"I think you've done a fine job."

Surveying the large room, she allowed, "I may run up some new curtains or throws to help blend your furnishings and mine. Together, we'll make it ours."

He came up behind her and settled his hands on her shoulders. "If you ask me, yours and mine are already a perfect blend."

His mouth was close to her temple, and Joanna felt his light breath stir the wispy bangs on her forehead. She snuggled into his hard strength, and his arms locked around her waist, pulling her tightly against him. For long moments she didn't speak. Content to be held, she contemplated the strange turns fortune can take. Three lives were about to change for the better. Hers, Scott's and Tony's.

Tony. The thought of her son brought on an attack of nerves. She didn't need the IQ of Einstein to measure how crazy her son was about Scott. But given his extreme sensitivity, she wanted to make sure they broke their marriage plans to him in exactly the right way.

She should have discussed her concern with Scott last night, but he'd kept her otherwise preoccupied. Then, before sunrise they'd softly tiptoed down the steps of the inn. Joanna had insisted upon stealth; she'd have been mortified if they'd run into one of the inn's employees. Much to her relief, no one had been sitting at the desk as they passed, and they'd been able to make their exit unobserved.

They weren't as fortunate on their return to the Hartman farm. John and Catherine were at the kitchen table, having an early breakfast, when the squeak of the front door had alerted Scott's mother to their entrance. "Who's there?" she'd called from the kitchen, a hint of panic in her voice.

"It's us, Mom."

"Scott? Joanna?" Turning on the hall light, Catherine had looked from one to the other, then opened her mouth to make an observation or ask a question— Joanna wasn't certain which—when John put a staying hand on her shoulder.

"We were just finishing up breakfast. I wanted to make an early start of milking so we could go to Sunday School. Would you like to join us for a cup of coffee? Or some cereal and toast?"

"Thanks, Dad. I don't think so."

Joanna had been amazed at Scott's blandness. Had he been such a hell-raiser as a youth that he'd become used to confronting his parents at this hour of the morning? Or was it that he simply knew them better than she did? Joanna couldn't prevent her face from blazing.

With a sigh, she put the awkwardness of that moment from her mind, aware that Scott had just spoken to her. "What was that?" she asked.

"I think it's time we talk with Tony. While I feed Miss Kitty, you can sell him on the place. Okay?"

* * *

"Sure is neat here, isn't it, Mom?" Tony noted a few minutes later. His hand was in his pocket, jiggling together the two quarters the tooth fairy had left him the night before.

He was starting to act like Scott, Joanna thought, touched by the masculine gesture that was so characteristic of his hero. Her precious boy was growing up, and in the years ahead he would need a father's guidance. How fortunate for them both that Scott was willing to fill that role.

Suddenly the shadows that had for so long darkened Joanna's heart lifted. "It certainly is," she agreed. Dominating one end of the large living room was a stone fireplace, reaching from floor to ceiling. At the other a leather sofa and two chairs had been carefully arranged to fill in the empty spaces, yet encourage conversation. An oak coffee table, end tables and lamps completed the grouping.

Joanna was struck by how much the house resembled the man. Solid and sturdy and dependable. Things you could count on for years to come.

Striving for a casual tone, she asked, "How would you like to live here?"

Tony's eyes drifted covetously to the large fireplace. Joanna could well imagine what was running through his mind—roasting hot dogs, toasting marshmallows. "I'd like it fine."

"Like what?" Scott inquired as he came back into the room.

"To live here."

Scott's smile was expansive. "Then your mother's already told you we're getting married."

Joanna's heart did crazy somersaults when the color drained from Tony's face. "N-not yet."

"Uh-oh. I hope I haven't put my foot in it."

"Not really. As a matter of fact, I was about to but—" she smiled brightly, nervously "—I hadn't quite gotten that far."

"Well, what do you say, sport? Would you like to be my best man at the wedding?" Scott didn't wait for an answer but extended a hand. "Come on, I'll show you around. You can pick out the room you'd like. Personally, I prefer the one at the end of the hall. It looks onto the back yard. There're some nice-sized maples and sweet gums out there just begging to be climbed."

"Don't put ideas in his head," Joanna warned, trying to maintain some semblance of normalcy. "We don't want any broken limbs. And I'm not referring to the trees."

"Funny lady." Scott tossed her a grin over his shoulder. "For a growing boy, climbing trees is as natural as breathing. Right, Tony?" He turned the doorknob and gave a push, revealing a room about three times the size of the one in their apartment. "So what do you think?"

When Tony didn't respond, Joanna's heart sank. With all his questions, Scott was digging himself into a deeper and deeper hole. In his happiness, his keen sensitivity to others had apparently abandoned him. He was as oblivious to Tony's silence as a deaf man to thunder.

Although her son's face gave away nothing, Joanna sensed his mounting anxiety and tried to ease the situation. "Your bed will fit nicely along that wall. Your dresser and bookcase here. And look at all the storage!" She gestured toward the four sliding doors opposite her. "You shouldn't have any trouble finding space for your toys."

"This is the ideal corner for a computer. Maybe Santa will bring us one." Scott curved an arm around Tony's shoulder and winked confidentially. "Don't tell any of your classmates, but their principal is a video-game junkie. How about you?"

When the question went unanswered, Scott glanced down at Tony. It was as if he'd only now taken notice of the boy's reticence.

Concerned eyes flew to Joanna's, but all she could offer was a shrug and a weak smile. "Tony," she said mildly, "you haven't answered Scott."

Looking up, he blurted, "Are you going to roll around in bed with my mom?"

"Tony!"

"Kathy told me that's what married people do." Without prompting, he went on, "Once, after school, I watched a soap with her. This man plopped this woman down on a bed, then they started rolling round and round. You always tell me not to bounce on my bed 'cause it's hard on the springs. So I thought they were bad to do that."

Embarrassed, Joanna blustered, "What did Kathy say?"

"She said they weren't being bad, they were sleeping together. But that didn't make sense. Their eyes were wide open." Tony's forehead creased. "She told me I wouldn't understand, but to take her word for it and that it was okay 'cause they were married." His gaze returned to Scott, and he repeated, "Are you going to sleep like that with my mom?"

Unable to contain his amusement, Scott rocked back on his heels and let his laughter fill the house. "I sure am. Right in there. But I promise, we'll be careful of the bed springs."

"Won't you ever shut your eyes and sleep like me?" Tony asked, sounding perplexed.

Scott gave Joanna a look and stooped down in front of Tony. "Sure," he answered. "But you don't close your eyes and lie real still every minute you're in your bed, do you?"

While Scott handled Tony's endless questions, Joanna's mind was elsewhere. Having Scott by her side to help deal with these knotty problems was going to be a godsend—especially when Tony reached dating age. She wouldn't have to face the awesome responsibility of playing father as well as mother to a growing boy.

Joanna was observing the two men in her life when Scott rose to his feet and asked, "Would you like some supper? I'm not as adept in the kitchen—" his eyes captured Joanna's "—as in certain other rooms in the house. But I do wield a pretty mean can opener."

"I could be talked into something light. But Tony looks bushed, so I'll leave it up to him. What do you think, honey? Would you like to stay for supper?"

At Tony's shrug of acceptance, Scott led them into the kitchen.

He hadn't exaggerated. His culinary skills were nothing to brag about. He opened cans of soup and heated hot dogs, but to Joanna it wouldn't have made any difference if he'd placed a juicy filet mignon in front of her. Her whole body was tense.

Throughout the meal she monitored her son for further signs of retreat. But he responded with some enthusiasm to Scott's pleasant conversation and even asked if he really thought Santa might come through with a computer. After a while Joanna began to relax.

Her spirits were further lightened when Scott phoned his parents. Joanna listened in on the extension and heard Catherine and John say how thrilled they'd be to set additional places for the holiday dinners. When they learned Joanna's parents would be in town for Christmas, they insisted the Mansfields also join them.

She was nearly moved to tears by their warmth, especially their enthusiasm over gaining a new grandson. How different from the Parkers, who had given her such a cold reception and whose interest in Tony was anémic at best.

By the time Scott drove them back to their apartment, it was close to eight o'clock, and Joanna had regained her euphoria. Everything was going to work out fine. Just fine. Already she felt a part of the Hartman clan.

Quickly she shooed Tony off to bed, listening to his prayers before tucking the covers up under his chin.

"Good night, honey," she murmured as she planted kisses on both cheeks. "I'll see you in the morning."

"'Night, Mom." When she reached over to snap off the bed lamp, he snaked a hand from beneath the covers and touched her arm. "Mom?"

"Yes?"

He gave a slight shake of his head. "Nothing."

A pleat of concern creased Joanna's forehead. "It must be something. What's on your mind, Tony?"

"Is Coach Hartman really going to be my dad?"

"Yes, he is."

"What should I call him?"

Relieved to discover that was all he had on his mind, Joanna said, "For now, Scott would be fine, though at school you'd better stick to Coach. After we're married, maybe you'd like to call him Dad."

Tony turned his face to the wall. "Okay."

Joanna smoothed the hair across his brow and gave him another kiss. "Sleep well, my little man."

When she returned to the living room, Scott was nowhere to be seen. She found him in the kitchen, putting on a pot of coffee. "And what, might I ask, do you think you're doing?"

"Perking some brew."

"Don't tell me you need a caffeine fix."

"Nope." He looped an arm around her waist and dragged her to him. "The only fix I need is you."

Joanna watched as his mouth swooped down to capture hers. She had no idea how long they stood in the kitchen wrapped in each other's arms, but by the time they broke for air, the percolator was no longer making gurgling sounds.

"Coffee's ready," she mumbled against his neck.

With obvious reluctance he let her go and opened the cabinet above the stove to retrieve two cups.

"None for me, thanks," Joanna said. "If I have coffee, I'll never fall asleep tonight."

Scott gave her a devilish look. "That has interesting possibilities."

Joanna laughed. "You're wicked."

"Wrong. I'm in love." He tugged her back into his arms for another languid kiss.

In the living room, they took seats on the sofa. Joanna kicked off her shoes, curled her feet under her and burrowed into the nest Scott made in the hollow of his arm.

"Let's talk wedding," he suggested. "We need to set the date."

"If—as you insist—we're to get married before Christmas, there're only five Saturdays to choose from."

"Pick one."

"Why me?"

"Don't be coy, woman. I thought you'd want to consider the time of month."

The smile she sent his way was anything but coy. "Naturally, there is *that* little matter, but what about you? Any extra obligations that we need to plan around? Like tons of board meetings, conventions or conferences to sap your energy? I wouldn't want my bridegroom so exhausted he couldn't live up to his husbandly duties.''

"Never fear. I could swim the Atlantic, climb Mount Everest, hike the Oregon Trail—all in a single day—but one look at you would rejuvenate me. And all significant body parts.''

"How shocking!''

"But you love it! Come on, admit it, my prim and proper fiancée,'' he coaxed.

"Hah! I'll agree to proper. But prim!'' She lifted her chin. "I think I'm offended.''

"Don't be. I like it when you loosen up. Now give me a wedding date.'' His voiced lowered. "So I can loosen you up some more.''

Smiling, Joanna leaned over and fingered the buttons on his shirt. "Let's make it, hmm-mm—'' she did some rapid mental calculations "—Saturday, December 12. That should give me time to send out the invitations, arrange for music, flowers and food for the reception, as well as buy a dress, shoes—''

"I thought we were keeping this simple?''

"The only thing simpler would be to elope.''

"I'm game if you are. I want us married, Jo. I don't care how, so long as it's soon. I want my ring on your finger. I want to start making babies with you. I want—''

Joanna placed two fingers against his lips. "I want those things, too. But we have other people to consider—your family, mine. And Tony. We have to give him a while to get used to the idea we're going to be a family. He's already wondering what he should call you."

"How about Dad?"

"That's what I said, but for now I suggested Scott. Maybe you'd like to talk to him about it. I don't have to tell you he'll be needing even more of your attention. He doesn't handle big changes in his life very well. But I'm hopeful he's secure enough now to take it all in stride." Her eyebrows pulled together. "At first I wasn't so sure. He was acting strange, but I think it was shock. You and I . . . well, it has happened rather fast. Five weeks—that's not too much to ask, is it?"

"Of course not." He ran a palm up the length of her thigh and over her hip to her waist. "If you're still keyed up, I know the perfect way to help you relax. And maybe get a head start on a family?" His fingers slid under the bottom of her loose-fitting sweater.

Joanna struggled to hold onto her reason. "You want children right away?"

He rubbed his hand lower and lower over her bare midriff until he touched the snap of her low-slung jeans. "Umm-hmm. Don't you think Tony needs a little brother or sister?"

Joanna longed to know the joy of having Scott's baby growing inside her. But for the moment all she could think about was feeling *him* inside her.

Reality retreated further and further with each pass of his hand over her heated flesh. Well into the night Scott made slow, tender love to her. As again and again their bodies melded and soared, they knew the supreme joy of oneness.

For Scott it was immensely gratifying that the face in the gold metal frame no longer stood in its place of honor on Joanna's bedside table. He took it as proof that there would never again be a ghost from the past to haunt him.

After dinner the following Wednesday evening, Joanna was washing up odds and ends that wouldn't go into the dishwasher. As she pulled her hands out of the water, the diamond on the third finger of her left hand winked at her.

Dreamily, she rinsed off the soap and inspected the stone. It was so large she considered it just this side of gaudy. Well, perhaps that was an exaggeration, but she'd never thought to own any piece of jewelry so magnificent. She would have been happy with a plain gold wedding band, but Scott had wanted her to have a diamond as well—even though their engagement would last but a few weeks.

On Tuesday, Joanna had taken off work an hour early so they could select the invitations and shop for her dress. At first she'd refused to allow Scott to help her with that particular task, since it was bad luck for the groom to see the bride in her gown before the wedding. But the imploring look he'd given her would have charmed the devil himself. Curbing her superstitious bent, she'd let him come along.

After paring her choices down to two, she'd tried them on. The first was a tailored yellow linen with a lace inset at the bodice. The other could only be described as a pink piece of froth. When she'd appeared in the linen, Scott's eyes had ranged over her appreciatively. But when she pirouetted before him in the chiffon, they'd smoldered. And so her choice had turned out to be no choice at all.

Joanna released the kitchen stopper and dried her hands on a towel. If she didn't stop mooning around, she'd waste the entire evening. Reaching for the phone, she punched in the Jacksons' number.

"What can I do for the future Mrs. Hartman?" Beverly asked.

"I need your advice. On bakeries and musicians."

"Grossman's and Nolan Evans. I'm surprised to hear from you. I thought you'd be out with that handsome hunk of a fiancé."

"He has a board meeting, but he promised to drop by later."

"Did you get hold of your parents yet?"

"Late last night," Joanna informed her. "They'd been on a tour of the Grand Canyon. Mom was ecstatic. She kept rattling on about how any woman choosing to live without a man must be crazy."

"When it comes to daughters, most mothers are of the same opinion."

Laughing, Joanna ended the call and dropped the phone back into the cradle. A glance at the clock told her it was well past seven. If her son were to make his eight o'clock bedtime, she'd better hustle him into the tub.

Walking down the hallway, she pushed open the partially closed door to his room. Joanna's heart nearly stopped beating. Tony was on the bed, lining up his chess pieces for battle.

On shaky legs, she moved across the room and sat down beside him. When the mattress tilted under her weight, most of the pieces toppled over.

"Ah, Mom!" Tony complained without looking up.

"I'm sorry, honey. What were you doing?"

"Playing."

"Why with the chess pieces?"

"'Cause."

"Because why?"

"They're fun."

"No other reason."

He shook his head.

"Well, it's time to put them away for tonight."

Before she got to her feet, Tony asked, "Mom, where'd your picture of Dad go?"

If he'd slapped her across the face, his question couldn't have created greater havoc. She paused, groping for the right words to explain what was going on in her life. Their lives.

"Tony," she began, "I'm marrying Scott. He's going to be my husband now, and to—to keep a picture of your daddy out in plain sight would be...awkward. It might make Scott think I didn't love him enough."

"Don't you love my dad anymore?"

"I'll always love him." She lifted a palm to caress his cheek. "He was your daddy, and that makes him very special. But he's—" *He's dead,* she was about to say but couldn't bring herself to utter the words. They sounded so hollow, so cruel. "Your daddy's gone, Tony."

"I know. He's in heaven."

"That's right, sweetheart. And as much as we miss him, we have to accept that he can't be here for us. He can't take you to ball games, he can't play with you." She smiled reassuringly. "But we have Scott now. Lucky for us, huh?"

Tony's frown brought tears to Joanna's eyes, and she drew him into her arms. "I understand how bewildering all this is. But trust me. We're going to be very happy together," she said, gently rocking him back and forth.

After he was in bed, Joanna nearly wore a path in her carpet. She didn't like Tony's renewed absorption with the chessmen and wondered what was really bothering her son. Had he again turned resentful?

As soon as the notion popped into Joanna's mind, she dismissed it. After their inauspicious beginning, Scott and Tony had grown close. They were such buddies she'd once experienced a pang of jealousy watching them together.

Joanna stopped in her tracks. Of course! Tony was *jealous*! He'd been doing some observing of his own, and he resented the attention she and Scott had been showering on each other.

Now that she understood, she almost laughed out loud. What a demon jealousy was! First she was jealous of Tony and Scott, and now Tony was jealous of the two of them! Or maybe he was simply jealous of her. Perhaps Tony considered Scott his friend and his alone. Perhaps he didn't want to share Scott's time and attention with his mother.

Joanna vowed to have a talk with her son tomorrow. She'd explain the different kinds of love, especially between a man and a woman and a parent and a child. For a while she and Scott might have to bend over backward to help Tony see how he fit into the scheme of things, but she was certain that together they'd work things out.

By the time Scott arrived, Joanna was feeling immeasurably better. She greeted him with an enthusiasm that knocked the wind from his lungs, at once giving herself up to the oblivion that his kisses always brought.

Little did she know that through a minute crack, a pair of eyes watched. Then a pair of hands eased the door closed, shutting out the happy scene.

Joanna awakened well before the alarm sounded. She didn't bother reaching out to search the other side of the bed. Even half asleep, she knew she would find it empty. By mutual consent, Scott never spent more than part of the night with her.

She preferred that Tony not find them together the following morning. She hadn't had to explain; Scott had understood.

As she threw back the covers, she winced from the cramps in her lower abdomen. No doubt her redheaded sister from Detroit—her mother's euphemism for a woman's monthly cycle—was about to pay her a visit. A few days early. Which was understandable,

Joanna allowed, given the emotional roller coaster she'd been riding the past few weeks.

In a way it saddened her because she and Scott hadn't already started a baby, particularly when neither of them was getting any younger. In the spring she'd turn thirty-one, and Scott was already thirty-eight. But, she thought with a reckless smile, she was certainly looking forward to trying again next month.

Joanna showered, dressed and had breakfast on the table before she wakened Tony. Juice had been poured, cereal bowls filled and bread toasted when she walked down the hall.

Nothing that morning had alerted her to anything being amiss until she entered Tony's room. As usual, his bed was a mess, the covers rumpled and askew.

But, uncharacteristically, her sleepyhead of a son wasn't beneath them.

She didn't have to search the bathroom or her own bedroom to know he was nowhere in the apartment. Even so, with her heart hammering in her ears, she gave both a hasty check, telling herself over and over that she had to be mistaken.

But she wasn't. Her son was gone.

Panic swamped her. Joanna flew to the phone and with trembling fingers punched out a number.

"Scott," she breathed into the receiver, her voice scarcely above a frantic whisper, "Tony's run away."

Chapter Thirteen

Fear clawed at Joanna as she and Scott climbed the steps to the police station. He kept a supporting arm around her waist until she collapsed onto a chair beside the desk of a man identified as Sergeant McElroy.

Mechanically, the officer inserted a form into his manual typewriter. "Your son's name?"

"Anthony Alan Parker. We call him Tony."

Using one finger, the man recorded the information with a speed that, under normal circumstances, would have astounded Joanna. But right now her life was far from ordinary.

Before he hit the last letter, McElroy fired a second question. "Age?"

"Six. His birthday was a few weeks ago."

"Hair color?"

"Light brown. With a slight reddish cast."

"Eyes?"

"Blue. Very bright."

"Blue," the sergeant noted.

Joanna shivered. How could he be so clinical, so impersonal? Tony was not a compilation of statistics but a dear little boy. Her precious son.

"Any clothing missing?"

"His coat—a red down jacket—and white sneakers. I—I didn't check for anything else."

"Any distinguishing marks—like a scar?"

"Yes." Joanna swallowed hard. Where did they expect to find her son. At the bottom of the Delaware River? "He has a dark mole on his shoulder."

"Left or right?"

"Left."

McElroy's finger froze above the typewriter. "His left? Or facing him?"

"Facing him."

"His right then."

"Yes, his right." Distractedly she pushed a hand through her hair. "It's on his right shoulder."

The sergeant hammered out the proper keys and ripped the missing person's form from his typewriter. "Sign here, ma'am."

Unsteadily, Joanna scribbled her name at the bottom. "Wh—what happens now?"

"We'll start at your building, interviewing neighbors. If that doesn't produce results, we'll widen the circle and keep on widening it till we find somebody who saw—" he swung the form around and glanced down "—Tony."

"We've already scoured the apartment complex," Scott said, "and talked to most of the neighbors, but no one's seen him. We even called the children in his class to find out if he said anything to them. Not even his best friend could tell us where he might be."

"Our officers are trained to probe for information that people don't know they have. It may seem like backtracking, but we could learn something you didn't."

Joanna let out a tattered breath. "How long will all this take?"

"No telling. We'll get your son's picture out and do our best."

As Joanna rose, Scott took her elbow. "What should I do?"

"Go back to your apartment. Little kids who run away—sometimes they don't go far. Maybe he'll come home on his own."

"And if he doesn't?" Joanna hadn't missed the lack of conviction in the sergeant's voice.

"Try not to worry. We'll take care of it."

Somehow the comment didn't inspire confidence, but Joanna was too dazed to press him further.

"Wait here," Scott softly ordered as they came out of the dreary station house. "I'll get the car."

Standing on the steps waiting for Scott, Joanna nearly gave into the hysteria that had been building since she'd discovered Tony missing. Turning to the police had seemed so final, a desperate admission that her son wasn't just playing a trick on her.

Joanna bit down hard on her bottom lip, drawing blood. She felt so helpless. But she had to keep her wits about her. For her own sake. For Tony's. If she tried hard enough, maybe she'd remember something that would provide a clue to his whereabouts.

She knew he'd left the apartment on his own, but what had happened to him in the meantime? He was so young, so little. Had a stranger kidnapped him? Had he hurt himself? Was he at this very moment lying bleeding somewhere? Crying for her? Alone? Frightened? Unable to summon help?

The toot of Scott's horn mercifully dissipated the painful images. But Joanna's sense of despair lingered. With feet as heavy as concrete blocks, she trudged down the steps.

For the next two days Joanna was unable to eat. She scarcely slept, except in fits and starts and never more than a few minutes at a time. Whenever the phone rang, she pounced on it with shaking hands. Was it good news or bad? Within her chest, hope seemed to wage an ongoing battle with foreboding.

Her parents kept in close touch, as did her sister, Lois, and friends from work. Beverly cancelled several obligations to stay with her. Then there were the daily contacts from Sergeant McElroy. Though the department was devoting a lot of man hours to the case, they hadn't turned up a single lead. It was as if Tony had disappeared from the face of the earth.

Scott spent all of Thursday with Joanna and left Whittier early Friday afternoon to rush to her side. Inwardly, she alternated between thanking him for letting her lean on his strength and cursing herself for ever becoming involved with him in the first place. By now she was certain Tony had fled because she and Scott were to be married.

She tortured herself with a thousand questions. Why hadn't she heeded the warning signs? Why hadn't she taken more care to reassure her son? How could she have been so insensitive?

Before long, she was in danger of collapsing. Yet she refused tranquilizers, arguing that she wanted to remain alert, ready to offer any help the police might need. By late Friday evening, however, her taut nerves rebelled, and she fell into a deep sleep while sitting upright on the hard-backed chair by her phone.

An old woman dressed as a gypsy, except for the black conical hat perched on her head, passed gnarled hands over a crystal ball. "I'll find him, Mrs. Parker," she boasted, her heavy accent punctuated by a cackle.

All at once Abby Wilson burst into the tent. Dripping wet in a scanty bikini, she pointed an accusing finger at Joanna. "That's what happens to man stealers. Their little hellions run away!"

"No, no, no!" a voice moaned. Her own? Hecate's?

"I almost had him," the fortune teller lamented. "But now he's gone." She bent closer to the foggy globe. "Aha! Good news. He's all right." Abruptly she vanished into thin air.

Moaning, Joanna stirred and tried to bring the old woman back. She'd been on the verge of revealing Tony's whereabouts. Joanna reached toward the vacant mist, but strong hands clamped down on her shoulders and held her back. Someone was shaking her. Abby again? No, the voice was too low. Maybe, Joanna considered dimly, it was Dwayne. He'd always said he was going to shake some sense into her. Or had that been someone else?

"Joanna . . . Joanna."

This time the sound seemed to be coming through a long tunnel, and she strained to hear it. Abruptly she sensed a presence hovering over her, felt the weight of warm fingers on her arms. Her eyes flew open and she catapulted to a sitting position.

For endless seconds Joanna didn't move, struggling to sort dream from reality. Little by little she began to realize she wasn't in a carnival tent but on her own bed with early morning light filtering through the window. How in heaven's name had she landed here? And why was she sleeping in her undergarments? The last thing she remembered, she'd been waiting fully clothed by the telephone.

A movement at her side claimed her attention. It took a moment for her brain to discern that Scott was there with her. And that his face was split by a happy grin.

"We have news, darling."

As his words penetrated her consciousness, she clutched at his shirt. "News? About Tony?"

"Yes, sweetheart. They've found him."

"They've found him?" Joanna wanted to cry but she lacked the strength. "Is he . . . is he all right?"

"He's fine. He was at Chris's all the time."

"Chris's?" She slumped against the headboard and rubbed her face with both hands. "But Chris said he hadn't seen Tony."

"He was pledged to secrecy." Scott held out her robe as she swung her legs to the floor. "No one in the family realized Tony was in the house. But Mrs. Edwards got suspicious when she caught Chris raiding the refrigerator after every meal. To make a long story short, she started snooping and discovered Tony hiding out in Chris's room."

Joanna hugged her middle. "Oh, Scott, I'm so relieved."

"I know you are, darling. So am I." He pulled her into his arms. "Mrs. Edwards is walking Tony home. He should be here shortly."

Joanna looked up at Scott. Until that instant, she hadn't noticed the dark circles beneath his eyes. His hair was mussed, his shirt and slacks rumpled, his face shadowed by his unshaven beard. He must have sat up all night agonizing over Tony. His concern touched her heart. And at the same time made it ache.

Now she had a second crisis to face.

Reluctantly Joanna disengaged herself from Scott's arms. "Before Tony gets back, we need to talk."

Filled with guilt and remorse, she led him to the living room. She should have leveled with him as soon as Tony disappeared, but she'd been too distraught to think straight. Still, ever since her son had run away, Joanna knew she had no other option.

Her throat tightened painfully. She was torn between her love for Scott and her love for Tony. But as a mother, she was bound to duty. Scott was a grown man who could fend for himself, but Tony was still a helpless little boy who needed her.

When they were seated next to each other on the couch, Joanna lifted her left hand and slowly worked the diamond from her finger. Dying a little inside, she extended the ring and pressed it into Scott's palm.

He slanted bewildered eyes from his hand to Joanna. "What's this?"

"I can't marry you," she said in a racked whisper.

"What do you mean you can't marry me?"

"Scott," she began in a tremulous voice. How could she explain something she didn't quite grasp herself? "I didn't think about the consequences of our plans. You made me so happy—when I thought I'd never dare be happy again. I was so caught up in what we had together that I—I didn't consider Tony's feelings. I know now I've been terribly selfish. I've put my own needs before my son's."

"Jo, I admit we may have miscalculated the effect of our relationship on Tony. But to break off—that's crazy. If there's a problem, we can work it out."

The hurt in his eyes sliced like a knife through her heart. More than anything, she wanted to throw herself at him and take her chances. But she couldn't. Tony had to come first. Before her. Before Scott.

Frantically, she searched for a reason, any reason to make him leave. Now. This instant! If he knew how close she was to weakening, he'd never go. And she'd never have the strength to let him. As she saw it, the quickest cut was the kindest.

Her voice was husky with unshed tears. "It's this way, Scott. I promised myself that if I got Tony back safe and sound, I'd give you up."

"Is that all? Oh, Jo, under tremendous strain, people always try to plea bargain. With God. With themselves. But that isn't why Tony's coming back—because you made a rash promise when you were half out of your mind with fear."

"I know that."

"So? You're not breaking any law if you renege." When she failed to meet his gaze, Scott's features gradually hardened. "Oh, I get it. You needed me for support when the going was tough, but *after* you find out Tony's okay, you issue me my walking papers. You were right in the first place. You are selfish. Both ways *you* come out a winner." His eyes narrowed to angry slits. "But I wind up with nothing!"

"You've got it all wrong! I put it badly. What I'm trying to say is Tony's not ready for another change in his life."

Scott spit out a four-letter word that fairly blistered her ears. "You're so damned hung up on what you *believe* is best for Tony, so blasted uptight about right and wrong, that you don't have a rational thought in your head."

The accusation cut deep. Sure she was distressed. Who wouldn't be? But how dare he attack her devotion as a mother! She was willing to give up everything for Tony. Make any sacrifice! Hot tears stung her eyes, but Joanna blinked them back, taking refuge in anger. "That's unfair."

"Is it? Then why try so hard to shield Tony from anything the least bit difficult or unsettling? Why not show him that he can learn from change and grow stronger?" Scott balled a hand and scoured his cheek with the knuckles. "Isn't life just one stage, one transition after another? Children have to learn to accept and deal with that. It's what One-for-One's all about, what—"

"My mind's made up. You can't change it, Scott."

"God, Jo, don't you know how much I love that boy? How hard the past two days have been on me? He's like my own flesh and blood. Weeks ago I started thinking about him as my son."

The tears she'd been holding back threatened to spill over. "I'm only trying to do what I think is best."

A scornful laugh erupted from deep within Scott's throat. "Not from where I'm standing, you're not."

Joanna thought she'd explode from the crushing pain in her chest. It was all she could do to turn away and whisper, "I don't want to argue about it anymore. Please leave. Please!"

Wearily, Scott picked up his coat from where it lay in a heap on the couch. Before carrying Joanna to bed, he'd draped it over her while she'd caught a few odd moments of rest. Now, without a backward glance, he slung it over his shoulder and headed for the door. "I won't be back, Jo."

When he'd gone, she stood stock-still in the center of the living room. How long she remained rooted to the spot she couldn't have said. Not until a series of chimes sounded in her entryway was she roused from her misery. As she moved across the room, her heartache mingled with an overwhelming sense of joy. Tony was home!

Scarcely able to see through the blur of tears flooding her eyes, she flung open the door and clasped him to her. When at length her emotion was spent, she steadied herself and leaned away. "Tony, you gave me such a scare! Don't you ever do that again!"

His arms circled her neck in a fierce, repentant hug. "I won't, Mom."

"Do you know how frightened I was?"

"Mr. Edwards told me."

"And I think he made his point."

As Joanna glanced up and spied Chris's mother, embarrassment seized her. Undoubtedly the woman was curious about why her son had felt compelled to run away. "I want to thank you for bringing Tony home," Joanna said, getting to her feet. "Would you like to come in?"

"For a minute," the woman agreed, stepping past her. "I want you to know how these little devils pulled the whole thing off."

When the door had closed behind them, Mrs. Edwards volunteered, "On Thursday morning Tony caught Chris on our porch waiting for his car pool ride and told him he'd run away. My helpful son sneaked him up the stairs and into his room. Chris is so messy he knows I steer clear of the place except for Mondays, when I go in to shovel it out." She rubbed Tony's sandy head. "As for this one, he was as quiet as a mouse. And as clever. Would you believe he didn't go to the bathroom unless he heard the vacuum or knew I was out on an errand? Bob gave both boys a sharp dressing down. I don't think they'll be causing us any more trouble."

"I hope not. I have a few things to say to Tony myself."

Mrs. Edwards reached for the doorknob. "I'm sure you do."

Joanna smiled. "Thanks again. And thank your husband for me, too."

After Mrs. Edwards left, Joanna took Tony's hand and steered him to the couch. "Sit down, young man."

"I'd like to go to my room."

"Don't be in such a rush," she said sternly. "You'll get a chance to spend plenty of time there later. Because you're grounded until next year!" Joanna couldn't remember ever being this strict with her son, but then he'd probably scared two decades off her life.

"Next year!" he protested.

"Don't look so horrified. It's only a matter of weeks until January. That's a light sentence for all the grief you caused me. And everyone else who loves you."

"I'm sorry."

Moved by her son's bowed head and tearful eyes, Joanna softened her tone. "Why did you run away?"

Tony shifted uneasily. Seconds ticked by while Joanna waited for his answer. Finally, he blurted, "I didn't think you wanted me anymore."

"Why?" she asked softly.

"You threw away Dad's picture."

Joanna was taken aback. "I didn't throw it away, honey. I merely put it in a drawer."

"You got rid of it."

Brushing the hair off his forehead, she reflected that it may be too late for her and Scott, but she needed to make her son understand. "Tony, I loved your father. Very much. He'll always hold a place in my heart. You often remind me of him, you know. You have his eyes.

And those reddish streaks in your hair—they're like Mike's."

"They are?"

Joanna nodded. "And sometimes when you smile, it's just the way your father smiled. But Daddy's gone, honey, and I'm still alive.... I'm only thirty years old. To you that must seem ancient, but when you're my age, you'll realize it's pretty young." Her expression grew wistful. "Your father wouldn't have wanted me to spend the rest of my life alone, any more than I would have wanted him to if... well, if I'd gone before him." She put an arm around Tony's shoulder. "To be honest, after your daddy I never thought I'd find someone I'd care about, someone I'd want to marry. Until I met Scott. Even so, I don't love him more than your father. Or you. I just love him in a different way. Can you understand that?"

"No."

"You will as you grow older." She gave him a squeeze. "I think you can understand this. I love Scott, but I'm not going to marry him. I broke our engagement. See?" She lifted her ringless left hand.

"We're not going to live with Scott?"

"No. He won't be coming to see us again, either. I wouldn't do anything that would make you so unhappy you'd want to run away. That," she said in a raspy voice, "is how much you mean to me."

For the first time since he'd returned home, Tony met his mother's eyes. The scowl that creased his forehead puzzled Joanna. She thought he'd be delighted by her news. But his face wasn't at all animated. What, she wondered, could be running through that six-year-old mind?

At the moment, though, she was too tired to pursue it. She'd give him time to think about what she'd said, and they could pick up their talk later when both of them were fresh. "Tony, I'm going to call your grandparents, Aunt Lois and everyone else who's been so concerned about you. After that, I want to lie down for a bit. I'll arrange for Kathy to come over and stay with you."

"I'll be okay by myself."

"No!" she answered too quickly.

From her bedroom Joanna put in two brief calls, one to Sergeant McElroy, the second to the Jacksons. Afterward she phoned her parents, telling them the good news about Tony and the unhappy news that there would be no wedding. Her mother didn't deny that she was disappointed. Though she advised Joanna against making hasty decisions, she didn't lecture, and Joanna was grateful.

By the time she'd notified the last person on her list, Kathy had Tony occupied in front of the TV. The muffled tones were reassuring rather than disturbing. Wearily she climbed beneath the bed covers and closed her eyes. Despite the ache in her breast, she'd expected to fall asleep right away. But even as exhausted as she was, she lay awake and stared at the ceiling.

One tear, then two leaked from the corners of her eyes. Within seconds a veritable storm had broken, and she rolled over, muffling her sobs in the pillow.

* * *

The next week was pure torture, and Joanna hadn't the energy to hide her despair. At work, she found herself out of sorts with everyone.

"Darlene!"

"What now?"

"I need those figures. An hour ago."

"Right, boss!" Darlene snapped, clearly miffed.

Around the house, Joanna was no better.

"Kathy?"

"Yes, Mrs. Parker."

"Turn that television down. My head is splitting."

"Yes, ma'am."

"And, Tony?"

"Whatcha want, Mom?"

"Pick up your room. It's a mess. You're getting as bad as Chris."

"I am not! I'm gonna clean it. As soon as this program's over."

"Now!"

Joanna sat at her neighbor's kitchen table, her chin propped in her palms. "I can't seem to control myself. In the past week I've been abrupt with everybody."

"That's not what I heard," Beverly revealed.

"Oh?" Joanna's eyes widened in disbelief.

"You haven't been abrupt, my friend. You've been downright nasty."

"Nasty! Isn't that a little harsh?"

"Not according to my sources."

"Sources?"

"Kathy and Tony."

At the mention of her son's name, Joanna's face crumpled. "I'm driving him away, aren't I?"

Beverly raised a shoulder. "Could be."

"And after—" She broke off.

"Giving up Scott," Beverly finished for her. "Joanna, why did you call off the wedding?"

"Tony ran away because he believed I didn't love him. He thought I loved Scott more. I considered it best all around that we break up."

"Growing up without a father. You think that's good for Tony?"

"Of course I don't, but you know how he is about anything different in his life." She inclined her head. "Now I'm not so sure I did the right thing. Lately he's been kind of morose. And I'm miserable."

Beverly leaned forward. "I hope what I'm about to tell you doesn't make you mad. But I believe you have a right to know. Tony's been talking to Kathy. He's afraid to tell you something."

"Afraid?" Joanna was about to take exception, but deep down she knew her friend might be right. She had been grouchy and unapproachable since Scott had walked out of her life. "What's the problem?"

"Tony's upset that Scott isn't going to be his father."

"What!"

"Maybe I should back up a bit. He told Kathy what you'd said about love. How what you felt for his father wasn't the same as what you felt for him, but that you loved them both. He thought you were making it up. But Kathy assured him you weren't. She said she loved her parents, but not the same way she loves Phil."

"Phil? I thought she was in love with Bradley."

"That was two weeks ago. Anyhow, as I was saying, Kathy quizzed Tony about the people he loved. Naturally, he said you and your parents. When he named Kathy, she probed a bit further—permit me to say I'm quite proud of the way my daughter handled this—and asked if Tony loved her the same way he loved you and his grandma and grandpa."

"And?"

"His exact words were 'That's crazy. You're just my friend.' And then, Kathy claimed his face lit up as if a light bulb had flicked on in his head. Want to know who else he told Kathy he loved?" She didn't wait for an answer. "Scott. You know what, Joanna? It's my guess he didn't run away because he wanted you to reject Scott. He was simply jealous. He's too young to understand love expands the more we share it. He thought there wouldn't be enough to go around."

"Strange. I suspected he might be jealous, but I had it figured wrong. I thought he considered Scott his personal property. My God," Joanna said dismally, "what have I done?"

"Made a hell of a mess. But—" Beverly grinned "—you can still undo it."

Joanna shook her head. "When Scott left, he told me in so many words that was it. He even said I was too uptight to be a good mother. He's always teased me about being conventional, but that hurt."

"Well, prove him wrong." Beverly's eyes gleamed with purpose. "I know the perfect way. That is, if

you're daring enough to take the bull by the horns."
She leaned closer and whispered in Joanna's ear.

Joanna gasped, then laughed for the first time in
days. "I could be arrested!"

"Possibly, but what a way to prove a point!" Beverly's hands went to her hips. "Come on, Joanna. For
once in your life, forge your own destiny."

Joanna waited outside Whittier's administrative of-
fices, fingering the shiny penny she'd found the first
day she'd met Scott. By accident she'd run across it in
the zippered compartment of her purse and considered it a good omen.

She'd been standing in the hall close to fifteen minutes when Scott's secretary finally emerged. The instant the woman turned a corner, Joanna scurried
across the polished floor, slipped inside and made her
way to the door marked PRINCIPAL.

She dragged in a long breath and blew it out to
steady her nerves. One hand clutched the lapels of her
coat, while the other quietly turned the knob. Slowly,
she pushed the door open a crack and peeked inside
before easing her body through the narrow gap.

To her relief, Scott's chair was turned so that his
back was to her. With quivering fingers she located the
lock and soundlessly turned it until she heard a slight
click.

Leaning against the door for support, she summoned up her sexiest voice. "Hello, Scott."

Like a shot he was out of his chair and facing her.
When he saw who it was, surprise vanished to be re-

placed by irritation. "If you're here in your capacity as a parent, I'll talk to you. If not—"

"I didn't come to see you as Tony's mother."

"Then you can leave," he announced bluntly.

"No, I can't." Joanna thrust out her lower lip in what she hoped was a seductive pout. "I was sent to the principal's office because I've been a very naughty girl."

Scott didn't utter a word, merely stared at her through slitted eyes.

"And I'm here to take my punishment." Slowly she unbuttoned her coat and slipped it from her shoulders.

"My God," he rasped.

She took a tiny step toward him, then another and another until she was within an arm's length. Provocatively she skimmed both palms down her body. "You told me I was too inhibited. As you can see, I could use some help...unwinding."

"Uh-uh, I think I *do see* through your little scheme." The beginnings of a smile played at the edges of his mouth.

"I hope so." She sighed heavily. "You have no idea how difficult it is to find a plastic wrap suitable for a strapless dress. I must have tried a dozen different brands."

"I didn't know there were that many on the market."

"It's amazing what you can uncover when you're desperate."

His eyes raked over her. "Obviously."

She lifted a hand to his shirt, then slowly walked her index and middle fingers downward from button to button. "But I'm ready to take my medicine. What'll it be, Mr. Principal?" she asked sweetly. "Ten licks with the paddle?"

"I have a better idea," he murmured, dragging her into his arms. "On the blackboard, write 'I love Scott Hartman' ten million times—so you're not apt to forget it."

"Fair enough, but that could take quite a while. I'll have to hang around school for years and years."

"I figured as much. That's why I'm giving you detention. For life."

Joanna sighed heavily. "Well, if that's what it takes." She stood on tiptoe and banded her arms around his neck. "But first, let's play hooky."

Scott grinned. "You read my mind. If I didn't know better, I'd swear you were taking lessons from that gypsy friend of yours."

"Does that mean you find me bewitching?"

"I find you damned irresistible, and if you don't cover up soon, I'm not going to be responsible for my actions." He picked up Joanna's coat from where she'd dropped it on the floor and hurriedly bundled her into it.

Giving her a quick once-over, he allowed, "That's better, but I notice the third finger on your left hand looks a bit bare." From his pocket he produced her engagement ring and slipped it into place.

"You still have it?"

"I couldn't bring myself to take it back. Carrying it around somehow made me feel closer to you."

"Oh, Scott," she cried, again throwing her arms around his neck.

The kiss was deep and long and healing. When Scott's control threatened to break, he set Joanna apart. "God, I missed you! Come on!" Grabbing his own coat, he nudged her through the door, announcing to his startled secretary, "Phyllis, I won't be back until this afternoon."

Joanna's brow puckered doubtfully.

"Make that tomorrow morning. I've got something...under wraps I have to check out."

* * * * *

The tradition continues this month as Silhouette presents its fifth annual Christmas collection

SILHOUETTE *Christmas* STORIES 1990

The romance of Christmas sparkles in four enchanting stories written by some of your favorite Silhouette authors:

Ann Major * SANTA'S SPECIAL MIRACLE
Rita Rainville * LIGHTS OUT!
Lindsay McKenna * ALWAYS AND FOREVER
Kathleen Creighton * THE MYSTERIOUS GIFT

Spend the holidays with Silhouette and discover the special magic of falling in love in this heartwarming Christmas collection.

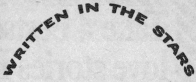
WRITTEN IN THE STARS

Star-crossed lovers?
Or a match made in heaven?

Why are some heroes strong and silent...and others charming and cheerful? The answer is WRITTEN IN THE STARS!

Coming each month in 1991, Silhouette Romance presents you with a special love story written by one of your favorite authors—highlighting the hero's astrological sign! From January's sensible Capricorn to December's disarming Sagittarius, you'll meet a dozen dazzling and distinct heroes.

Twelve heavenly heroes...twelve wonderful Silhouette Romances destined to delight you. Look for one WRITTEN IN THE STARS title every month throughout 1991—only from Silhouette Romance.

STAR

Silhouette Books®

Take 4 bestselling love stories FREE

Plus get a FREE surprise gift!

Special Limited-time Offer

Silhouette Reader Service®

Mail to
In the U.S.
3010 Walden Avenue
P.O. Box 1867
Buffalo, N.Y. 14269-1867

In Canada
P.O. Box 609
Fort Erie, Ontario
L2A 5X3

YES! Please send me 4 free Silhouette Special Edition® novels and my free surprise gift. Then send me 6 brand-new novels every month, which I will receive months before they appear in bookstores. Bill me at the low price of $2.74* each—a savings of 21¢ apiece off cover prices. There are no shipping, handling or other hidden costs. I understand that accepting the books and gift places me under no obligation ever to buy any books. I can always return a shipment and cancel at any time. Even if I never buy another book from Silhouette, the 4 free books and the surprise gift are mine to keep forever.
*Offer slightly different in Canada—$2.74 per book plus 69¢ per shipment for delivery. Sales tax applicable in N.Y.

335 BPA 8178 (CAN)

235 BPA R1YY (US)

Name	(PLEASE PRINT)
Address	Apt. No.
City	State/Prov. Zip/Postal Code

This offer is limited to one order per household and not valid to present Silhouette Special Edition® subscribers. Terms and prices are subject to change.

© 1990 Harlequin Enterprises Limited

Win 1 of 10 Romantic Vacations and Earn Valuable Travel Coupons Worth up to $1,000!

Inside every Harlequin or Silhouette book during September, October and November, you will find a PASSPORT TO ROMANCE that could take you around the world.

By sending us the official entry form available at your favorite retail store, you will automatically be entered in the PASSPORT TO ROMANCE sweepstakes, which could win you a star-studded London Show Tour, a Carribean Cruise, a fabulous tour of France, a sun-drenched visit to Hawaii, a Mediterranean Cruise or a wander through Britain's historical castles. The more entry forms you send in, the better your chances of winning!

In addition to your chances of winning a fabulous vacation for two, valuable travel discounts on hotels, cruises, car rentals and restaurants can be yours by submitting an offer certificate (available at retail stores) properly completed with proofs-of-purchase from any specially marked PASSPORT TO ROMANCE Harlequin® or Silhouette® book. The more proofs-of-purchase you collect, the higher the value of travel coupons received!

For details on your PASSPORT TO ROMANCE, look for information at your favorite retail store or send a self-addressed stamped envelope to:

PASSPORT TO ROMANCE
P.O. Box 621
Fort Erie, Ontario L2A 5X3

                      3-CSSE-3

ONE PROOF-OF-PURCHASE

To collect your free coupon booklet you must include the necessary number of proofs-of-purchase with a properly completed offer certificate available in retail stores or from the above address.